Suddenly While Gardening

Two days later the Pollards returned to London, making an early start and arriving home by lunchtime. The afternoon was fully occupied in unpacking, and it was not until he was relaxing over a cuppa at teatime that Pollard picked up the evening paper.

'Good Lord! Just look at this!'

On the front page, under the caption 'MODERN SKELETON IN ANCIENT MONUMENT', was a recognisable photograph of Davina Grant and himself standing beside the Starbarrow kistvaen. 'Detective-Chief Superintendent Tom Pollard on a hiking holiday stumbles on a macabre mystery and a pretty girl,' he read.

Other titles in the Walker British Mystery series:

ELIZABETH
LEMARCHAND

Suddenly While Gardening

WALKER AND COMPANY · NEW YORK

First published in the United States of America in 1978 by the
Walker Publishing Company, Inc.

This paperback edition first published in 1983.

ISBN: 0-8027-3005-1

Library of Congress Catalog Card Number: 78-67180

Printed in the United States of America

10 9 8 7 6 5 4 3 2 1

To
Robert W. Fynn
and
William G. Hoskins

Chief Characters

DAVINA GRANT	of Upway Manor, Glintshire
PETER GRANT	architect, her brother, also of Upway Manor
MRS BROOM	their daily help
GEOFFREY LING	retired, of Starbarrow Farm
KATE LING	his daughter
GEORGE AKERMAN	owner of Letterpress, a printing works, and secretary of the Friends of Cattesmoor
ROBERT DELL	horologist
ISABEL DENNIS	aunt to Detective-Chief Superintendent Tom Pollard and committee member of the Friends of Cattesmoor
HENRY LANDFEAR	Chief Constable of Glintshire
DETECTIVE-SUPERINTENDENT WILLIAM CROOKSHANK	of the Glintshire CID
DETECTIVE-CHIEF SUPER-INTENDENT TOM POLLARD	of New Scotland Yard
DETECTIVE-INSPECTOR GREGORY TOYE	of New Scotland Yard

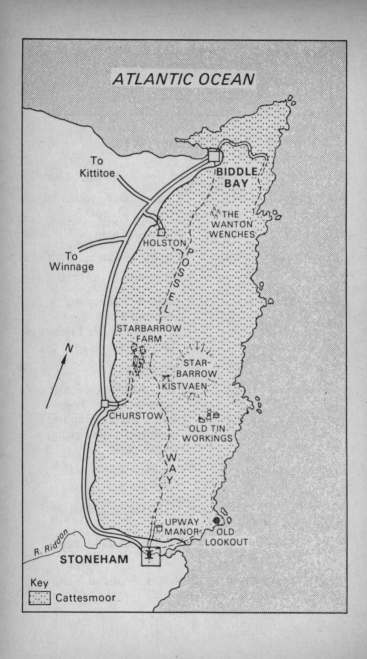

Chapter 1

Detective-Chief Superintendent Tom Pollard leant on the garden gate of his aunt's cottage, watching the June day burn itself out over the Atlantic. Life felt good. His promotion was still recent enough to keep recurring agreeably to his mind. During the day he had successfully transported his family down from London for a fortnight's holiday, and no essential clobber had been left behind. The record fine spell showed no signs of breaking up. He had enjoyed his supper, and would shortly stroll down to the congenial village pub with his wife Jane, leaving good old Aunt Is to babysit. Not that she'd have any bother. Andrew and Rose, the six-year-old twins, had been dead to the world within minutes of climbing into their bunk beds. Tomorrow they'd all have a super day at . . .

Distant footsteps attracted his attention. Two tired sloggers, he interpreted. Not heavyweights. A couple of young hikers, perhaps. He turned his head in the direction of the path coming down from Cattesmoor to the village of Holston, and a few moments later two boys of about sixteen emerged, very sunburnt, dusty and sweaty, but trudging doggedly.

'Hullo,' Pollard said, as they approached. 'You look as though you've done a mile or two.'

'Cuh! Twen-ty-sev-en ruddy miles,' the more forthcoming of the pair told him. 'We've done the whole Possel Way since breakfast.'

'Good Lord!' Pollard exclaimed, genuinely impressed. 'What time did you start?'

'Half seven. It's one of our school's options for after O Levels. All you can say is the others are worse, aren't they, Blotch?'

The second boy, in less good shape, had slumped thankfully against the wall, and nodded without speaking. Then he suddenly straightened up, letting off a yell.

'Hiya, Dad! Where's the car, for Pete's sake?'

9

'Here at the pub,' a man shouted from further down the street. 'Keep going, chaps!'

With a hurried farewell to Pollard the boys started off again with renewed energy. He watched them, an idea taking shape in his mind, and then turned to go back into the cottage. As he did so, his aunt's telephone rang. He by-passed the sitting room where she was taking the call, and joined his wife in the kitchen.

'I wonder if she'll be long?' Jane Pollard said. 'Perhaps I'd better hold up the coffee.'

They stood listening. A flow of gratified comments interspersed with questions came from the sitting room.

'Somebody's pulled off something to do with one of her pet ploys, from the sound of it,' Pollard diagnosed.

After a brief interval Isabel Dennis rang off and appeared in the doorway, a small energetic figure in dark slacks and immaculate blouse, her eyes alight with triumph.

'We – the Friends of Cattesmoor, that is – have won our Possel right-of-way case,' she announced. 'The judge awarded us costs, too. That was George Akerman, our secretary. He's ringing round to all the committee.'

'What exactly *is* this Possel Way, Aunt?' Pollard asked her.

'It's a medieval pilgrim route along Cattesmoor to Biddle Bay, dear. They used to embark there for Compostella. "Possel" is probably a corruption of "Apostle", referring to St James, of course ... Jane, how good of you to make the coffee. Bring the tray into the sitting room, Tom, and I'll show you some maps.'

On the inch-to-a-mile Ordnance Survey map a footpath was intermittently marked from west of Stoneham to the seaside resort of Biddle Bay. Isabel Dennis explained that the Friends of Cattesmoor had wanted for years to clear it and make it accessible to walkers, but lack of funds had made this impossible.

'You see,' she explained, 'we have to carry on a practically non-stop running fight with the water and electricity people, and commercial interests like afforestation and quarrying. They simply couldn't care less about conserving one of our few remaining sizeable open spaces with all its beauty and interest. It costs us the earth to be represented at public enquiries, and there's next to nothing left for the things we want to do. But quite out of the blue last year we had a legacy of £5,000 from our late Chairman, Heloise Grant. Such a tragedy: she was killed by a fall from a ladder, poor dear. But I can't pretend that the legacy wasn't marvellous for the Friends. With all that in the kitty we got the backing of the Ministry of the Environment and the County Council, and went ahead with Possel at last.'

'Did you manage to find the original track over the whole distance?' Pollard asked.

'Yes. We got unexpected help over that. There's a firm that does air photography which got interested, and saw advertisement possibilities. They sent a helicopter and photographed the whole area for free. It's amazing how things show up from the air, isn't it? After that it was a question of clearance, and restoring some footbridges, and way marking. A big job, but the work went splendidly. A lot of volunteers came forward. And now this right-of-way business is through, the job's done.'

'Was it a farmer digging his toes in?' Jane asked from the window seat.

'No. If it had been, one might have had some sympathy. Some walkers are a perfect menace: completely irresponsible. It was a tiresome selfish man called Ling. He bought Starbarrow Farm which was no longer occupied, modernised it, and moved in three years ago ... You can see it better on this larger scale map, Tom. Just below Starbarrow, one of the high bits of Cattesmoor, with tumuli on the top. The enclosure behind the farm buildings is Starbarrow newtake. It was enclosed in 1756, perfectly legally, but the man who did it got away with building a drystone wall all round it, blocking the Possel Way which ran straight through it, quite close to the house.'

'And this Ling fellow took the line that possession was nine points of the law?'

'Exactly. Of course the row didn't start up until quite recently: not long before Heloise Grant's death, in fact. Up till then there was no real prospect of reopening Possel. For one thing we hadn't the money, and for another there was no surviving *written* evidence that the track originally ran through Starbarrow newtake, although part of an old chapel is built into one of the farm's barns, and we felt certain that it had been used by the pilgrims. Then a simply incredible thing happened . . . More coffee, either of you?'

'Do go on,' Pollard said, getting up to collect Jane's cup. 'I can't wait to hear what it was. Did St James of Compostella oblige with a miracle, or something?'

'Well, it really seemed like one,' Isabel Dennis replied, inspecting the contents of the coffee pot. 'An historian who was doing some research in the Vatican archives came quite by chance on a document about Possel. It was a petition in medieval Latin for pilgrims using the Way to and from Compostella to be granted an Indulgence for praying in the chapel of St James at Starbarrow. "Sturberow", it was called, but the location was quite clear. The man who found the document happened to know our county archivist, and sent him a photostat. Heloise Grant was thrilled, and told the Friends' General Committee that she'd anticipate the legacy she'd left us, and put up the money for Possel right away. Ling was informed, and replied that he couldn't care less about the document. He threatened to prosecute if any attempt was made to clear a path through his newtake, which had reverted to over-grown moorland, by the way. Then shortly after this Heloise died. The legacy came to us, and after we'd taken legal advice we decided to go to court on a right of way issue.'

'Why was Ling so bloodyminded?' Pollard asked.

'He's a most extraordinary man. Hardly sane, I should have thought. He said he'd searched England for a really secluded house where he could get peace and quiet in his old age, and wasn't going to have a lot of yobs and trippers disturbing him.'

'It's secluded all right,' Pollard said, looking at the map. 'There isn't even a road to it.'

'No. You get there by a track up from Churstow on the Biddle–Stoneham road, and then drive across open moor. The Lings have a Land Rover.'

Jane Pollard eyed her husband quizzically.

'When do you start?' she asked.

'For Compostella?'

'No, darling. To walk the Possel Way.'

'What? Me walk twenty-seven miles? You must be joking!'

'Aren't Chief Supers expected to keep fit like Other Ranks? You can tone up the muscles by doing some training hikes first. Anyway, you'd practically decided to go when you came in from talking to those boys, hadn't you?'

Pollard admitted that something of the sort had passed through his mind.

'Will Ling take a pot shot at me?' he asked his aunt.

'Unlikely,' she replied. 'He was livid in court and got ticked off by the judge, but seems to realise that he's got to give in. He's insisting on clearing the track through his newtake himself, and putting up barbed wire on each side. It will look awful, but save us expense, of course ... There's no problem at all about your doing the walk, Tom. I'll give you a really early breakfast, and one of us can run you over to Stoneham. You'll easily get back here in time for supper.'

What the household called Pollard's Assault on the Possel Way took place on the last day but one of the holiday. Isabel Dennis laid on a substantial breakfast at half-past six, preparatory to getting him to Stoneham well before eight o'clock. In the event their departure was held up by an unexpected uproar from the twins. Rose wept bitterly, convinced that she was never going to see her father again, while Andrew protested with angry roars that he could walk miles and miles, and they were beastly not to let him go too. At last comparative calm was restored, and Pollard leapt into the waiting car.

'Sorry about this fracas, Aunt,' he said. 'One thing, they're still young enough to be quite easily distracted.'

Isabel Dennis agreed. 'When I get back we'll take them down to the beach with a picnic lunch,' she said. 'Then we'll all have a hot meal tonight when you turn up.'

'Today's Great Thought. I can see it keeping me going when my legs start giving way under me. Thank the Lord it's cooler than last week.'

'There's always a breeze up on Cattesmoor. You've got an ideal day, I should think.'

They came out on to the Biddle Bay–Stoneham road, and headed south-eastwards. On their left, behind the great mass of Cattesmoor, the sun was flooding a cloudless sky with the clear golden light of morning. A light mist was dispersing rapidly from the fields. At this early hour there was little traffic, and Isabel Dennis made good time, only slowing down to pass through an occasional village.

'There isn't a single road crossing the moor from south to north, is there?' Pollard asked presently.

'No. The lanes running up from the villages peter out beyond the fields on the lower slopes. They're just for getting stock up and down. All these parishes have grazing rights on the moor. You see, there's no coast road on the north side. Just a sheer drop down, and great gullies running into the land. There's a path of a sort for part of the way, but it's very rough going. Look, there's Stoneham in the distance. We're not much behind time.'

'Can we steer clear of police H.Q.? I don't want to be spotted by Crookshank or any of his chaps, and have to start reminiscing about old times,' Pollard said, referring to a previous case in the area.

'Easily. We needn't go through the middle of the town at all.'

They took a devious route through the outskirts of Stoneham, and arrived in a rather drab and old-fashioned working-class district.

'Here's where you start off,' Isabel Dennis said, drawing up at the kerb. 'Pilgrim Lane's first left. Follow your nose till you get clear of the houses, and you'll see our signpost where the road starts going up to Cattesmoor. After that the track's marked right through to Biddle. You can't miss it. Have a good day. I'm just going to do a little shopping and then go straight back.'

'Well, thanks most awfully, Aunt,' Pollard said, getting out. 'Jolly good of you to ferry me over at this hour. If I don't turn up by midnight, send out a rescue party, that's all.'

He grinned and waved her off. As he stood adjusting his rucksack a clock chimed the half-hour. He grasped his stick and bore left into Pilgrim Lane which turned out to be a rather dreary little street, its original rural character long buried under the bricks and mortar of Stoneham's expansion. At the moment it seemed crowded with children. He edged past a string of small ones being escorted to school by two young mums in jeans who were conversing volubly. A stream of older boys and girls were progressing in the same direction, shouting to make themselves heard above the general tumult. Farther on a brisk trade in fruit and vegetables was being carried on from a small van with its nearside wheels on the pavement. Looking rather out of place, a red B.M.W. driven by a young man drove past cautiously, making for the town centre. An upper window went up with a screech and a mop was vigorously shaken out by an elderly woman. A postman, zigzagging briskly from one side of the street to another, gave Pollard a brief appraising glance and a friendly jerk of the head.

The type of house changed farther along Pilgrim Lane, marking successive stages in the town's growth. The solid little eighteenth-century stone houses gave way to hideous terraces of red brick dwellings. These ended in allotments and an untidy builder's yard, beyond which was an estate of small bungalows with gardens, and a bridge over the river Riddon. Cheered by the view of the eastern slopes of Cattesmoor ahead, Pollard pressed on, keeping in to the side of the road on hearing a car coming up behind him. It was the B.M.W. again. As it overtook him he saw that the driver had collected a passenger, a woman wearing a dark overall and holding a shopping bag on her lap, doubtless a domestic helper fetched from the town. He watched the car go up the hill and suddenly turn off to the right, towards a house just visible among some trees. It reappeared almost at once on its return journey, and on passing Pollard once again the driver raised a hand in salute. Shortly afterwards Pollard reached the signpost mentioned by Isabel Dennis. It pointed up the hill, indicating that Biddle Bay was twenty-seven miles distant; it bore the inscription THE POSSEL WAY, and a cockle shell, the pilgrim's symbol.

About halfway up the hill he reached the point at which the car had turned off the road. A pair of handsome wrought-iron gates stood open. They were supported by two stone pillars, one of which carried a board with the name of the house, Upway Manor. Pollard took a few steps inside, and looked down a gravelled track to a roomy garage containing a single car. The main drive curved to the left between tall rhododendron bushes. He went along it for a short distance, and found himself facing just the type of small country house that appealed to him most. It was simply and solidly built of grey stone, silvery in the morning sunlight, two-storied, and with pairs of long windows on either side of a porch supported by slender pillars. Four shallow steps led up to the front door. Above the parapet small dormer windows added interest to the hipped roof. Red climbing roses had been carefully trained over the south-facing façade and were in full bloom. As a woman's figure passed quickly across one of the bedroom windows he drew back a little, and turned his attention to the garden. It had been imaginatively laid out and the display of roses was magnificent, but there was a suggestion of current neglect. Weeds had sprung up in the drive, and the grass edges badly needed trimming. With a final envious glance at the house Pollard retraced his steps, reminding himself that he had a long way to go.

Immediately above Upway Manor the tarmac surface of the road ended abruptly. For a time a deep stony lane ran between high hedges laced with wild roses and honeysuckle and frothing with Queen Anne's Lace. The air was full of summer scents, and he breathed it in with enjoyment. Gradually the hedges dwindled away and the rough lane became a grassy track. He arrived at the top of a steep rise and came out on the open moor.

It gave the impression of stretching to infinity, a vast expanse of greens, yellows and browns studded with great grey rocks, while overhead was an immense sky, unbroken by a single cloud. Pollard had an immediate disturbing sense of being utterly alone, isolated from the rest of humanity and dependent solely on his own resources. The impression faded as swiftly as it had come, leaving him amused at himself, and reflecting that he had become over-conditioned to urban life. He extracted the Friends of Cattesmoor's pamphlet, *The Possel Way*, and sat down on a flat rock to refresh his memory. It was conveniently divided into sections, giving the mileage of each and listing features of special interest. He decided on a rough timetable and set off westward with easy swinging strides.

On the rough grass the track was barely distinguishable, but there were bare patches where the bedrock which the pilgrims must have trodden was exposed. A waymark with its cockle shell symbol indicated a path cleared through an expanse of bracken which came up almost to Pollard's shoulders. He snapped off a piece to serve as a fly whisk as he passed. A couple of miles or so farther on he reached one of the Friends' major clearances, this time through a large impenetrable jungle of gorse bushes, brambles and leggy heather. On coming out on the far side the track began to drop down to a steep-sided little valley which he had earmarked as a suitable spot for a brief halt and some elevenses. He froze in his tracks as a heron floated up between the trees, and with incomparable grace moved downstream with slow dignified beats of its great wings. He watched it out of sight and went down the sharp drop, glad of the chance of some shade. The stream was very low, brown peaty water flecked with sunlight creeping quietly round the stones in its bed. An ancient clapper bridge consisting of a single huge flat stone spanned the water. Pollard sat on it, his legs just clearing the stream, and munched an apple. He left the spot reluctantly, aware that time was getting on and that he had barely covered a quarter of his journey. Another four miles would get him to Starbarrow, where he planned to have his lunch break.

As he swung along he toyed with the idea of doing the walk again the following year, this time with some sort of portable camping gear. It was maddening not to have time for detours to look at hut circles and a stone row described as 'exceptionally fine'. But the silence, broken only by lark song filtering down and the occasional lowing of cattle, had an hypnotic effect on him. His mind seemed to drift happily from one topic to another without reaching any conclusions.

Eventually another waymark indicated the best route through a rocky expanse forming the approach to Starbarrow. Suddenly realising that he was hungry, Pollard began to look out for a comfortable lunch spot. He rounded a large boulder and stopped dead. Fifty yards ahead of him, and farther up the slope, was a group of

17

about a dozen people of both sexes and varied ages, equipped with rucksacks, cameras and binoculars. Their attitudes unmistakably expressed alarm and indecision. Two of them, a youngish woman and a grey-headed man, appeared to be having an argument. Another man caught sight of him and interrupted them. All heads were turned in his direction.

He walked forward.

'Anything the matter?' he called, recognising with foreboding an authoritative note in his voice.

It was obvious that others had recognised it as well. Most of the faces confronting him were expressing relief at the prospect of pushing responsibility on to someone ready to take it. The argumentative young woman, however, looked slightly annoyed.

'Only a stupid practical joke,' she said shortly. 'Some idiot's put a skeleton in this kistvaen. It's a Bronze Age grave.'

She turned and indicated a box-like stone structure formed by stone slabs on their edges with one acting as a lid. Its overall measurements were roughly five feet by four.

'Students,' someone remarked with finality.

'That's right,' said an elderly woman. 'Keep saying they can't live on their grants, but all of them have cars, and go tearing all over the country.'

The grey-headed man contrived to catch Pollard's eye warningly.

'May I have a look?' Without waiting for an answer, Pollard advanced on the kistvaen. One of the upright slabs of stone was broken. He knelt on the grass and peered through the opening. After a prolonged scrutiny he got to his feet again.

'This is a police matter,' he said. 'The Stoneham station must be notified at once. Where's the nearest telephone?'

'Really!' the young woman retorted, now clearly very angry. 'I've no idea who you are, but this party is on a guided walk led by me, and I'm the one to decide what's to be done. The Friends of Cattesmoor are responsible for the Possel Way and the prehistoric monuments along it, and the proper person to notify about this – this outrageous nonsense is their Secretary, Mr Akerman. He's the person

18

to decide what steps to take, as the Chairman's in America. I shall—'

'Good Lord!' the grey-headed man interrupted. 'You *are* the police! Superintendent Pollard of Scotland Yard, isn't it? I remember your photograph in the local rag when you were on that murder case over at Kittitoe a few years ago.'

There was a sudden buzz of conversation.

'Unfortunately I am a policeman,' Pollard replied, 'and, please note, I'm on holiday. My only responsibility is to see that the Stoneham police are notified about this business as soon as possible. Is there a telephone at the farm down there?'

The young woman hastily climbed down with a rather forced smile.

'Of course this quite alters the situation, doesn't it?' she enquired of no one in particular. 'Yes, there is one, but the man who lives there is quite capable of refusing to let us use it.'

'I hardly think he'll go to those lengths,' Pollard replied, writing a few lines on a piece of paper and signing them. 'Will somebody take this note down to him, and then ring the police station at Stoneham to report what has happened? I must stay here myself until they turn up.'

The young woman immediately volunteered, refused the offer of a companion, and hurried off. Several plaintive voices enquired if everybody had got to hang around until the police came. It transpired that the walkers had come out from Stoneham by bus along the road to Biddle Bay, getting out at a village called Cobbacott, and cutting up across the moor to the Possel Way, which they were to follow back to Stoneham.

Pollard decided to take their names and addresses and let them go on. The grey-headed man who had actually discovered the skeleton contrived to be the last in the queue. He gave his name as Bill Worth.

'I'm an artist,' he said. 'Address: 2, Hill Crest, Stoneham. I was the first to find the thing because I was walking on ahead and went to have a look at the kistvaen. Of course I saw at once that it wasn't a bit of lecture room equipment, just as you did. It isn't wired up, and it's white – obviously a pretty recent vintage. But Miss Grant, who's leading this walk, and everybody else immediately concluded that it had been dumped there as a student rag, and I was being shouted down when you providentially turned up.'

'Did you say Grant? Is she related to a Miss Grant who was Chairman of the Friends of Cattesmoor, and died recently?'

'Yes, a niece. She and her brother both lived with their aunt, and have been left the house. A lovely little Queen Anne affair called Upway Manor. You must have noticed the gates on the way up to the moor. Miss Grant senior was a sort of local queen-pin, and fanatically keen on conservation and whatever. The niece – Davina, she's called – is obviously trying her hardest to step into her aunt's shoes, and is finding them several sizes too large. Hence the weight-throwing, which won't have escaped your notice . . . I say, this is really rather an odd business, isn't it? Somebody not only getting hold of a comparatively recent skeleton, but managing to land it here, miles from anywhere. Except Starbarrow Farm, of course.'

Pollard declined to be drawn. 'I expect the Stoneham chaps will manage to sort it out. I shall report to them that you actually found the skeleton, and they'll get on to you at an early stage, of course. In the meantime I'm sure you'll agree that discretion's called for. Here's Miss Grant coming back.'

'I'd better push on, then,' Bill Worth said reluctantly. 'Nice to have met you in the flesh.'

Davina Grant seemed anxious to give the impression of being briskly competent. Mr Ling had been out, and his wife had made no difficulty about letting her use the telephone. The Stoneham police were coming out at once, and should be on the spot within an hour.

'I directed them to come up here through Starbarrow Farm,' she said. 'It's much the shortest way.'

Pollard detected a note of satisfaction in her voice.

'I understand that Mr Ling objected to the Possel Way going through his land,' he said conversationally.

'He behaved abominably . . .'

As she talked, Pollard observed her critically. Somewhere in her late twenties, he thought, and quite attractive.

20

She had a rounded face with rather full cheeks, good hazel eyes and attractively styled dark hair. A small, rather secretive mouth suggested the tension that the artist had talked about. Presently he cut into the recital of Mr Ling's iniquities.

'I mustn't delay you,' he said. 'Your party has gone on, but they'll be expecting you to catch them up for the rest of the walk.'

'Won't the police want to see me?' she asked in obvious disappointment.

'Probably they will, but I can let them have your address.'

'They'll know that, of course. Upway Manor.'

Pollard thanked her, and solemnly added it to his list.

As soon as she had gone off he fell on his long overdue picnic lunch with relish, and afterwards strolled down to inspect the right-of-way through the Starbarrow newtake. A narrow path barely allowing walkers to pass across it in single file had been clumsily fenced with a great deal of barbed wire. Still, he thought, the Friends of Cattesmoor would probably be only too thankful to leave it at that. He returned to the neighbourhood of the kistvaen, and lay down comfortably on springy heather, propping his head against his rucksack. It was maddening, he thought, to have got caught up in this affair. Somehow he must get a message phoned through to Holston. He was damned if he would give up the Possel Walk, having got this far . . .

He awoke with a start to find a dark man with a large nose gazing down at him, a glint of amusement on his saturnine face.

'Caught you napping, Chief Superintendent Pollard,' remarked the new arrival. 'Not a thing I'd ever have expected to do.'

'Well, I'm blowed,' Pollard exclaimed, struggling to his feet. 'Superintendent Crookshank!'

They shook hands, and briefly harked back to the Kittitoe case.

'Thought I'd come along myself for old times' sake,' Superintendent Crookshank said. 'What's all this about a skeleton up here?'

'Come and take a look,' Pollard invited . . .

As soon as he decently could he extricated himself, having given a concise account of his arrival on the scene and the steps he had taken, and handed over the names and addresses of the members of the guided walk.

'It's all yours,' he concluded. 'Now I'm off, two hours behind schedule. You'll see that one of your chaps rings that number I gave you, won't you?'

Crookshank, now confronted with a decidedly bizarre situation, was reluctant to let him go.

'Be seeing you, maybe,' he suggested.

'Not on your life,' Pollard retorted.

With a final wave of the hand he started off once more on the Possel Way.

Chapter 2

Two days later the Pollards returned to London, making an early start and arriving home by lunchtime. The afternoon was fully occupied in unpacking, and it was not until he was relaxing over a cuppa at teatime that Pollard picked up the evening paper.

'Good Lord! Just look at this!'

On the front page, under the caption 'MODERN SKELETON IN ANCIENT MONUMENT', was a recognisable photograph of Davina Grant and himself standing beside the Starbarrow kistvaen. 'Detective-Chief Superintendent Tom Pollard on a hiking holiday stumbles on a macabre mystery and a pretty girl,' he read.

'Surely not the Stoneham police?' Jane queried a couple of moments later.

'Almost certainly it's that know-all artist type, Worth. I remember he had a camera slung round his neck. I can just imagine him tooling off to the local press and spinning a good yarn. It's a damn nuisance, though. The A.C. will certainly react.'

'I don't see how you can be held responsible,' Jane began indignantly. 'You couldn't . . .'

The telephone bleeped, cutting her short. She answered

it and passed the receiver to her husband, mouthing 'The A.C.'s office.'

The Assistant Commissioner was crisp.

'I understand you're back, Pollard. Have you seen an evening paper?'

'Yes, sir,' Pollard replied. 'About three minutes ago.'

'I should like an explanation of how you come to be involved in this affair then.'

Pollard gave a succinct account of the events leading up to the taking of the photograph. The Assistant Commissioner listened in silence, and at its conclusion gave an audible sniff.

'Most unfortunate,' he commented. 'If you hadn't blundered into the business I don't believe for a moment that the Glintshire people would be trying to push the enquiry on to us.'

Pollard felt an odd sensation of having subconsciously known all along that he was by no means through with the Starbarrow skeleton. Why, he wondered, had he been so reluctant to face this? He was suddenly nettled by the A.C.'s attitude.

'I really don't see, sir, how I could help getting involved under the circumstances,' he protested.

'I'm not criticising the routine steps you took. I'm merely saying that it's unfortunate that you turned up at that particular moment.'

'I absolutely agree, sir. What reason is Glintshire giving for calling us in?'

'Apparently the skeleton doesn't match up with any recorded disappearance from their area, for one thing. Then they've clearly got cold feet. The chap was never buried, at least not in the usual sense of the word. Somebody must have stowed the body away about a year ago, and then for some reason decided to yank it out and dump it where it was bound to be discovered in a matter of days. Glintshire think they're up against a lunatic, and possibly a psychopath.'

Pollard asked if there were any signs of injury.

'None. A few of the smaller bones are missing. Lost in transit, presumably.'

There was a fairly lengthy pause, finally broken by the

A.C. clearing his throat decisively.

'Well, as I said, they've called us in, and asked for you to take over, on the grounds that you know them and the area from your Kittitoe case, and were involved in the discovery of the skeleton. You'd better go down with Toye tomorrow and look into things, I suppose. Only for God's sake get on with it, Pollard. You can't be spared to hang about for weeks if you feel you're getting nowhere. As you know very well, we're stretched to danger point up here.'

'I realise that, sir. I'll consider myself as doing a recce, and report back to you as soon as possible.'

The A.C. was sufficiently mollified to enquire into the success of the family holiday. He finally rang off, and the door opened to admit Jane's head.

'Was the A.C. perfectly foul?' she asked, coming into the room.

'A bit bloodyminded to start with, but he came off it, and even ended up with asking about our holiday. I think he was chiefly hipped because Glintshire have asked us to take over the enquiry, and put in a request for me. I'm to go down with Toye tomorrow.'

'Hardly worth coming home, was it? Still, there are worse places than Stoneham, I suppose.'

They both turned towards the door as the twins marched solemnly into the room wearing shorts and tee shirts, and with improvised rucksacks on their backs. They progressed round it and went out again, heading for the garden.

'What on earth are they doing?' Pollard asked.

'Walking the Possel Way,' Jane replied. 'It's the in game at the moment.'

He groaned and settled down to a stint of official telephoning. His first call was to Detective-Inspector Gregory Toye who had worked with him on all his big cases, and who, like himself, was due back from a fortnight's leave on the following day. Toye received the news of their immediate assignment to an enquiry out of London with equanimity.

'Nice part of the world down there,' he commented. 'What time will we be starting, sir?'

'What you really want to know, of course,' Pollard replied, 'is whether we're going by rail or road. Well, to keep you happy, we'd better make it road. We're likely to be coasting round a bit, I imagine.'

Toye, a superb driver with a passion for cars, remarked gloatingly that that would be the Rover, then.

'Hope you'll enjoy driving it across trackless moorland,' Pollard said. 'If you can bring your mind to bear on anything but the car, I'd like to get off at about seven tomorrow morning. I'll brief you on the way down.'

As they swept down the M4 in the early freshness of the following morning, Pollard roused himself with an effort from the enjoyment of being driven by Toye in a top car.

'Well, I'd better let you have what gen there is,' he said, and started on the potted history of the Possel Way. When he came to the end of the briefing he glanced round at Toye's pale attentive face, rendered additionally serious by a large pair of hornrimmed spectacles, and saw mental digestion in process.

'How far off the footpath is this kistvaen affair?' Toye asked presently.

'It's about fifty yards up the slope of Starbarrow. It's quite conspicuous, and mentioned in the Friends of Cattesmoor's pamphlet as a good specimen. The sort of people who'd be on the Posse' Way would almost certainly go up to have a look. I'd intended to myself. What I'm getting at is that I'm certain the skeleton can't have been there long. Somebody would have discovered it. And the bones seemed so – well, fresh, when I looked into the kistvaen. There were no spiders' webs on them, for instance.'

'I suppose the ground all round the kistvaen had been pretty well tramped over by the walking party?'

'Yes. I don't think Crookshank's boys will have found anything useful. It seems to me that to start with, our best bet is to try and find out when the skeleton was brought there. It simply must have been by night. According to my aunt, quite a lot of people are using the footpath, and by day you could never be sure that somebody wouldn't suddenly come round the corner, just as I did. And incidentally there was a full moon last Saturday. A public appeal to anyone who's visited the kistvaen during the past couple of weeks, say, might narrow down the period we've got to cover.'

'This artist chap Worth,' Toye said after an interval. 'Somebody wanted the skeleton found, and he found it, didn't he?'

'I've been thinking along those lines myself,' Pollard replied. 'I'm always a bit suspicious of these matey man-to-man blokes, and he was so careful to point out quite unnecessarily that Starbarrow Farm would have been a handy base for the dumping operation. We'll certainly enquire into Worth and his activities.'

'What beats me,' Toye said, 'is why a skeleton, which must have been tucked away safely for a year at least, should suddenly be thrown out where it was bound to be spotted.'

Pollard agreed that this was one of the rummest affairs that they had ever investigated, and that Stoneham's theory of some brand of crackpot might very well be the answer.

'Of course,' he went on, 'it's important not to be distracted by the skeleton from the little matter of when the poor bloke it belonged to departed this life, from natural causes or otherwise. The explanation of the whole business may lie there. However, one step at a time ... We're getting along a fair treat,' he added, looking at his watch. 'Crookshank said they'd expect us about eleven.'

Twenty minutes later they drew up in the familiar car park of Stoneham police station, and shortly afterwards were shown into Superintendent Crookshank's office, where Henry Landfear, Chief Constable of Glintshire, also awaited them. Pollard noted that he had lost a couple of stone since they last met, but that his habitual gloom had returned. Both men seemed harassed. He learnt that the news of the discovery of the skeleton had appeared in a special edition of the area's morning paper on the previous day, having apparently been leaked to the press too late for the normal edition. The information given was much the same as that in the London evening papers, but the nearness of Starbarrow Farm to the kistvaen had featured more prominently

'I suppose local people have got it in for this chap Ling who owns the farm, because of the row over the right of way?' Pollard asked. 'I heard all about it from my aunt

26

over at Holston.'

'His name's mud round here,' Henry Landfear replied. 'I don't suppose more than five per cent of the inhabitants of these parts will ever set foot on the Possel Way, but there's nothing like obstruction of a right of way for getting people simply hopping mad. After the court hearing Ling had to be escorted to his car. And now we're faced with the hell of a problem. Yesterday evening a gang of Stoneham youths – the usual trouble-makers – went out to Starbarrow Farm on their motor bikes and started a rough house. They came belting back here, saying they'd been fired on. The super sent a couple of his chaps out there, and Ling's story was that they'd tried to break in and threatened to burn the place down, and he'd fired a few shots over their heads. He went on to say that if they turned up again he'd aim lower. He wouldn't listen to reason or warnings, and flatly refused police protection, saying he was quite capable of looking after himself and his wife and property. Of course we're sending a couple of men with dogs along this evening without letting him know they're there, but God only knows how we can keep it up. We're desperately short-staffed, like everybody else.'

Pollard commiserated and agreed that if there were a viable case against Geoffrey Ling, the sooner he was pulled in the better for all concerned. He gave his opinion that the skeleton had been put into the kistvaen only shortly before it was discovered, and suggested that an appeal to recent walkers on the Starbarrow section of the Possel Way might narrow things down, and also provide a starting point for questioning Ling.

'There's also the question of whose skeleton it is,' he said, 'and whether the chap died down here or was brought here after his death. Has the pathologist been able to put together a rough description of what he looked like?'

Superintendent Crookshank produced the pathologist's report. Deceased had been between sixteen and twenty years of age, five feet six inches in height and of medium build, with bleached shoulder-length hair reverting to its natural dark brown colour at the roots. There were old fillings in three of his teeth, the latter having been neglected recently. There were no signs of bone injuries, but the fibula of the left leg and some of the metacarpals and metatarsals were missing. Death was estimated to have occurred between thirteen and sixteen months previously. Traces of various substances had been found on the skeleton. These included rust, glass, hemp fibre, sawdust and cement, and bacterial organisms associated with putrefaction. There were faint traces of blue-green algae characteristic of small areas of stagnant water containing an excess of decaying organic matter. The pathologist's guarded conclusion was that during the process of decomposition the body of the deceased had not been buried in earth, but apparently kept in a dark, damp and confined space, possibly an old junk store of some sort.

'Between thirteen and sixteen months ago,' Pollard said thoughtfully. 'That covers the spring and early summer of last year, and includes Easter. In an area like this it's a time when visitors, welcome and unwelcome, start turning up. Let's get another appeal out with the one about the kistvaen, asking if anyone remembers a youth of this age and description during that period. It's a pretty long shot, but they do come off now and again.'

Both appeals were drafted and a constable summoned over the inter-com to take them for immediate despatch to the broadcasting authorities and the press. Henry Landfear then reverted to the subject of Geoffrey Ling of Starbarrow Farm.

'You'll interview him, I take it?' he asked.

'I thought we might pay him a visit this afternoon,' Pollard replied. 'Can you fill in a bit? I understand he's fairly new to these parts.'

'I've never met him,' the chief constable said, heaving his still considerable bulk into a more comfortable position on his chair. 'My wife went to hear the right of way case – she's a Friend of Cattesmoor – and came back quite intrigued. He struck her as a chap who made a pose of eccentricity but was anything but a fool underneath. There's a rumour that he took a First in something or other, and makes up those crosswords with incomprehensible clues. I don't know where his money comes from, but there must be quite a bit around. Starbarrow Farm was more or less derelict, and people say he's done himself damn well. As you know, he's got this thing about privacy. A rum-looking bloke, my wife says, with one of those india-rubber faces like a stage contortionist.'

Pollard had a flashback to a treasured little rubber face with a blank expression which had been confiscated from him at school by an unfeeling art master. You squeezed it, and the underlip or the tongue would shoot out, or the eyes bulge or the mouth grin hideously ... He jerked himself back into the present, and asked if Mr Ling had any family.

'Yes, there's a wife and a daughter. The wife goes in for pottery and weaving and whatever, but she seems as allergic to ordinary social life as he is. They're reputed to have people to stay occasionally – old friends, I suppose – but never accept local invitations or entertain out there, although the girl's boy friends are on visiting terms. She's away most of the time in a job – a lectureship at a horticultural college near Wintlebury. A brainy girl and attractive, too, my wife says. Last Christmas she got engaged to a local lad, young Peter Grant, who's a junior partner in a Stoneham firm of architects.'

'Is he any relation to the Miss Davina Grant who was leading that guided walk when I got embroiled?' Pollard asked.

'He's her brother.'

'One more point, and we'll clear off and get some lunch before going out to the farm and bearding Ling. What sort of a chap is this Bill Worth who says he discovered the skeleton in the kistvaen?'

Henry Landfear looked enquiring. 'Says? Any reason to suppose he knew it was there?'

'Nothing you could call a reason. But he struck me as a bit anxious to brief me about this and that, and kept on ramming home how near the kistvaen is to Starbarrow Farm, in case I hadn't taken it in. And I did think it odd that a chap of his type was on a guided walk at all. Anybody with half an ounce of gump could have got hold of the Friends' pamphlet on the Possel Way, and gone on his own as I did myself. The rest of the party certainly weren't his cup of tea, and he was decidedly snooty about Davina Grant.'

'Any comment?' Henry Landfear asked Superintendent Crookshank.

'I reckon he went on the walk to get copy for his column in the *Advertiser*,' Crookshank replied, referring to the weekly newspaper published in Stoneham. 'He writes a piece each week on something that's of local interest. Quite good, but a bit malicious, a lot of people think. If he can make anyone look silly, he'll do it, like young Miss Grant trying to carry on everything her aunt did, and enjoying a change from second fiddle. Funny sort of bloke. Getting himself into print and his pictures into exhibitions makes him think he's a cut above the rest of us, from the look of it. But I can't see him getting mixed up in anything criminal. Certainly not a homicide.'

'We've nothing against him, have we?' Henry Landfear asked.

'Nothing at all bar his nuisance value, sir. He's one of these minor complaints chaps.'

'Obviously I made the mistake of not taking him at his own valuation last Monday,' Pollard said. "Hence the photograph and the jibe underneath, I suppose. Did you see it.'

They both had, and agreed that it was typical Bill Worth.

'Two birds with one stone,' Crookshank added. 'He got in a jab at Miss Grant as well, didn't he?'

'If you're going out to see Ling,' Henry Landfear said, 'we'd better rustle up a Land Rover for you, don't you think, Super? It's hardly a run for that classy outfit down in the car park. You go out on the road to Biddle Bay for about eight miles to a village called Churstow. Then turn right up a narrow lane past the church – here it is on the map, see? It soon turns into a rough track which peters out on Cattesmoor, but you can't miss your way. Follow the posts carrying the telephone cable. The ground's like iron after the long drought, but a bit bumpy, of course.'

'The Land Rover's made Inspector Toye's day,' Pollard told him. 'Can you get a car up on to the moor from the other villages on the Biddle road? If the skeleton didn't come from Starbarrow Farm, it must have been brought along somehow. A bit conspicuous just to sling it over your shoulder.'

After some discussion the two local men agreed that you could get a car up from any of the villages, but that it would be impossible to do it without being noticed. Superintendent Crookshank undertook to have enquiries made, and that these should cover strangers on horseback as well.

Over their lunch Pollard and Toye discussed tactics for the interview with Geoffrey Ling.

'We've nothing to go on at the moment,' Pollard said. 'It's simply to give us a chance to vet the chap himself and spy out the land. Keep it short, and Ling guessing, I think.'

They easily located Churstow and the turning up to Cattesmoor, and noted that about half a dozen people materialised in doorways to watch their progress up the steep narrow lane. Toye, who was enjoying himself in spite of his critical attitude to the Land Rover's standard of maintenance, carefully negotiated the deeply rutted surface beyond the cottages and the gateway giving on to the moor. Pollard shut the gate behind them and stood looking around him. Their route ahead climbed steadily through a great sweep of heather, in which the deep purple of the bell variety was giving place to the soft rose-pink of ling. The only sign of life was a kestrel poised almost motionless in the cloudless sky above them, and some distant white blobs of sheep moving slowly on a patch of greenness. He got into the car again and they started off along the faint wheel tracks following the telephone cable. Toye remarked that it must have cost a packet to get the G.P.O. to run a line out that far. Pollard agreed, studying the map closely as they progressed. After about a mile and a half he forecast that they would see the farm from the top of the next rise. A couple of minutes later they looked down on a cluster of grey buildings backed by a windbreak of trees, diminutive in the great stretches of the moor.

'Blimey!' Toye exclaimed. 'Talk about the world's end!'

Through binoculars Pollard could see a walled garden gay with flowers in front of the farm house, and what appeared to be a number of large notices. After a time these became legible. 'STRICTLY PRIVATE', 'KEEP OUT', 'BE-WARE OF THE DOGS', 'YOU HAVE BEEN WARNED', he read out. 'And unless I'm much mistaken, Ling's watching us coming along from over the top of the garden gate. Duck when you hear the whistle of bullets, won't you?'

Suddenly a loud booming filled the air, and a huge hollow voice informed them that if they were reporters they came at their own risk.

'Step on it,' Pollard ordered. A smart acceleration carried them over the intervening ground to a standstill, with the car's nose and the POLICE notice on the windscreen confronting the face looking over the gate. It was a red-brown weathered face under wisps of grizzled hair. As Pollard stared at it in fascinated recognition its underlip shot out truculently.

'Hooligans with threats of arson. A brace of police. The local police boss-man. High-ups from the Great Wen. Without a warrant you shall not set foot across my threshold.'

While these statements were being declaimed in an unexpectedly high and pedantic voice Pollard extricated himself from the car.

'Good afternoon, Mr Ling,' he said. 'We haven't time to cross your threshold this afternoon, so the matter doesn't arise. I am Detective-Superintendent Pollard of New Scotland Yard, and this is my assistant, Detective-Inspector Toye. We are conducting the official enquiry into the discovery of human remains in the kistvaen on Starbarrow.'

'Go ahead and prove that I put it there, then,' Geoffrey Ling invited. 'You'll have your work cut out.'

'Even Euclid needed data before proving a proposition,' Pollard replied. 'When was this house last unoccupied overnight?'

Geoffrey Ling cast up his eyes to heaven in mute appeal. Finally, as Pollard remained impassive, he stated that the last occasion had been for a few weeks at the end of March in the previous year.

'The police,' Pollard said, watching him, 'are interested in last Friday, Saturday and Sunday nights. Were you yourself in residence then?'

Just for a split second, before Geoffrey Ling's features were distorted into an expression of ironic gravity, there was the blankness of indecision.

'I was,' he replied.

32

'Did you at any time during these nights hear any sound such as a distant car or someone on horseback, or anyone moving about outside?'

'I did not.'

'What dogs have you got here?'

At the abrupt change of subject and tone Geoffrey Ling flung open the gate. A black and white cocker spaniel bitch tumbled out and squirmed excitely over Pollard's feet.

'The plural is a little touch of poetic licence, Superintendent, to discourage – er, callers.'

'How do you keep your rats down?' Pollard was surprised to hear himself asking.

For the first time Geoffrey Ling forbore to grimace and looked at him with interest.

'Can it be that a top cop from the Great Wen is – or once was – a countryman?' he enquired. 'Meet Attila, the Scourge of God, and Tamburlaine the Great.' With a wave of his hand he indicated two huge battle-scarred toms sunning themselves on the wall, one orange, and one white with a sinister black patch over its left eye. 'Cattesmoor, aptly named by its aboriginals the home of wild cats. We found these two here when we came.'

'This is Inspector Toye's line,' Pollard told him. 'He's hooked on cats. Go along and take a look, Toye. Well, Mr Ling, I don't think we need trouble you any further, at present, that is. If I could just put the question about those particular nights to your wife?'

'She heard nothing.'

'You must know, I'm sure, that we can only accept statements at first hand.'

An oddly gratified gleam appeared in Geoffrey Ling's light blue eyes. He raised his hand in a gesture enjoining silence. Muffled thuds were audible.

'Penelope! Leave your loom! An importunate suitor is without!' he carolled in a high-pitched cracked voice.

Mrs Ling was plump and placid, with straight light brown hair screwed into a bun. Not surprisingly, she was also sparing of speech.

'What is it?' she asked, eyeing Pollard with casual interest.

He stated his credentials and business, and repeated his

question about the previous Friday, Saturday and Sunday nights.

'I heard nothing,' she said. 'I wasn't here.'

As Toye, who had unobtrusively rejoined the group, took down the address at which she had been staying from Thursday evening to Monday morning, Geoffrey Ling gave a short bark of laughter.

'Just a moment,' Pollard said. 'Was your daughter at home on those nights, Mrs Ling?'

'Yes.'

'He who laughs last, laughs longest, I think, Mr Ling?' Pollard queried as Toye took down a second address. 'We shall, of course, be interviewing Miss Ling.'

'No, you can't see the kistvaen from the back windows of the house,' Toye reported, as they jolted gently over the moor. 'Not at this time of year, anyway. The trees are much too close. They pretty well block out any view on that side, and there are quite a few outbuildings, too. I hadn't time to look inside more than a couple. One had an electric pump in it, for the water, I take it, and the other was a wood store, full of logs. There's a back door, and I don't suppose they bother to lock it at night. Easy enough to slip out and disappear into the trees.'

'As far as the daughter goes,' Pollard said, 'I just can't believe that she wasn't out with young Grant at any rate on one night last weekend, and that would leave the field clear for Ling, of course.'

Toye agreed that it was a point.

'Ling knows something,' Pollard went on. 'I'm certain he does. If only somebody comes forward and swears that the skeleton wasn't in the kistvaen on Friday afternoon, we might consider bringing him in for questioning if nothing more turns up in the meantime. Anyway, it hasn't been a wasted trip. And I bet I know who's had the biggest kick out of it, too . . . Through Darkest Glintshire at the Wheel of a Land Rover?'

Toye declined to rise, merely remarking sedately that it made a nice change after the motorways. As they approached the gate leading to the lane down to Churstow a woman with grey hair accompanied by a wirehaired terrier

34

came through it. On catching sight of the car she waited, holding the gate open. Pollard leant out of the window to thank her.

'Local custom,' she told him, with a speculative look. 'Not that there's much occasion for it as a rule. It's only these last few days that the track's become a highway. Scotland Yard, isn't it? You're not our police, and obviously not the Press. I'm Elsa Fordham, a retired Churstow incomer, as we're called by the genuine villagers.'

Pollard introduced himself.

'I expect all the comings and goings have attracted quite a bit of interest,' he said tentatively.

'Coupled with the Starbarrow kistvaen they're likely to be the talking point of the century, I should think. One can hardly get inside the Woolpack these days. But I can tell you one thing.'

'And that is?' Pollard prompted.

'The bobby who arrived just now and is diligently calling at every house won't find out anything about cars going up and down. People will just clam up. It's a village that hangs together.'

Pollard considered the implications of this remark, and decided to come to the point.

'I shouldn't have thought that the owner of Starbarrow Farm would be reckoned as a member of the Churstow community.'

'You're wrong there. In an odd sort of way the village is quite proud of him as a well-known character. Incidentally, he's openhanded, and always pays on the nail. And then there's the Them and Us factor, stronger than ever since rural rates went up astronomically. That bobby is one of Them, you see, poking around at Our expense. The poor chap's had it before he even starts.'

Pollard laughed. 'I suppose you yourself haven't any helpful information about cars coming and going last weekend, for instance?'

Elsa Fordham shook her head.

'My husband and I are right out of it. We live in a small lane on the other side of the main road. Well, it's interesting to have met you. You're not a bit my mental image of a Scotland Yard detective . . . Goodbye – I'll shut the gate after you.'

'What the hell do people expect us to look like?' Pollard demanded, as they drove down the lane. 'Sherlock Holmes? I bet some of these locals could give you a pretty accurate list of the cars that have passed up and down during the past week. I saw a curtain drop back as we went by. Let's hope the bobby's smarter than Mrs Elsa Fordham obviously thinks.'

They turned out into the main road and headed for Stoneham.

Chapter 3

When enquiries into the past history of the Lings had been put in train, and the appeals for information put out on the early evening news critically listened to, Pollard felt at a loose end. There was not even the usual expedient of filling in time by having a good square meal. He agreed with Toye that the heat made the hotel dining room unthinkable, and after a drink and a snack at the bar they returned unenthusiastically to the police station to await possible developments.

Superintendent Crookshank was off duty, but they were greeted by Inspector Hemsworthy with the news that two calls had come in since the broadcast. One was obviously a hoax. The other caller had stated that he had visited the kistvaen on the Tuesday of the previous week and that there was no skeleton in it then. He had given his name and address.

'Better than nothing,' Pollard said, 'but too far back to be much use. I simply don't believe the skeleton was put in before the weekend.'

Inspector Hemsworthy agreed. In the room provided for the Yard team Toye made a note of the information, and in the absence of anything further to do they settled down to study the meagre data in the case file.

'Ling,' Pollard said presently, resting his chin on his hands. 'A lopsided type. Good brain – a retired academic of some sort, I should think. Why this eccentric buffoon act, I wonder? Is it because Nature's given him the face for it?'

'Could be,' Toye agreed. 'He'd have been a star turn on the box.'

'After going over there this afternoon,' Pollard went on, frowning as he spoke, 'it's perfectly easy to visualise him planting a skeleton in that kistvaen simply to annoy the Friends of Cattesmoor by involving the Possel Way in a lot of sensational publicity. Hitting back at them for taking the right of way dispute to court and winning hands down. The point is that it's the wrong sort of skeleton for a jape of that sort. Not an ancient wired-up affair borrowed from a college or a medical pal, but one that was walking around as recently as about a year ago decently clothed in flesh. And one whose owner seems to have spent the intervening post mortem period under unusual conditions, to say the least of it. Somehow I can't see Ling keeping a body in a glory hole for twelve months, and then suddenly chucking it out on a public path, nor killing the chap in the first place, come to that . . . Hell, we seem to have been over all this before, in one way or another.'

'Suppose,' Toye said slowly, 'the chap was a keen salesman or something, and turned up at the farm on chance. Ling might have hit the roof and uttered threats. Brought out a gun, perhaps, or even fired a shot like the other night. Suppose the chap had a weak heart and dropped down dead. That would account for there being no signs of bone injury. Ling knows he's got a dicey reputation locally, and bungs the body into one of those sheds. I know this doesn't explain why he – or somebody else – brought it out and dumped it in the kistvaen. But if something like this happened and we got a search warrant, there'd bound to be traces of the body. We'd have something to work on, then.'

Pollard thrust back his chair and clasped his hands behind his head.

'As things are at the moment I can't see that we've enough grounds to justify asking for a warrant. The only thing against Ling right now is that his house is the only one anywhere near the kistvaen. A suggestive fact if you like, but that's all, so far. You know, I'm beginning to feel that it's a mistake to concentrate so much on the kistvaen business. The roots of this affair are so much further back, right back to the dead chap himself: who he was, and what he was doing in these parts, or, if he was brought here after death, what local contact or contacts he had. That's what we ought to be getting down to, though God knows— Come in!'

Inspector Hemsworthy appeared, followed by a young constable.

'There's been another phone-call, Mr Pollard,' he said. 'This one's reliable all right: the rector of the parish church and his wife. They were walking on the Possel Way last Thursday, and had a look at the Starbarrow kistvaen about three o'clock. No sign of a skeleton then, or anything unusual. Then there's been an anonymous call which mayn't be anything to do with your enquiry, but as it was a bit out of the ordinary I've brought along Constable Jackman who was on the switchboard.'

Constable Jackman was a youthful-looking blond, at the moment bright pink and rigid with self-consciousness.

'Let's hear about it, my lad,' Pollard said encouragingly.

Relaxing slightly, the constable stated that when the call came through he had given the stock response: 'This is Stoneham Police Station.'

'Nobody spoke, sir, not for a second, say, and I was just starting to repeat what I'd said when a funny sort of voice said "AQW 227N", and then rang off sharp.'

'QW's a Glintshire car registration mark, as no doubt you gentlemen have noticed,' Inspector Hemsworthy took up. 'We've checked on AQW 227N, and it's a Stoneham car. A B.M.W. belonging to Mr Peter Grant of Upway Manor. It's a well-known local family. He's a partner in a firm of architects here. We couldn't trace the call. It was S.T.D.'

Pollard's good visual memory produced a series of pictures of the B.M.W. and its driver passing and repassing him as he made his way out of Stoneham on the previous Monday morning.

'A funny sort of voice,' he repeated. 'Do you mean a

38

disguised one, Constable?'

'That's right, sir. Not what you'd call natural. Very deep it was, and sort of hoarse.'

'A man's voice?'

Here Constable Jackman was less definite.

'I took it for a man's at the time, sir, but on thinking it over, I'm not a hundred per cent sure. I mean I couldn't swear to it.'

'This is the Mr Peter Grant who's engaged to Mr Ling's daughter, I take it?' Pollard asked Inspector Hemsworthy, who dismissed the constable with a jerk of his head, and sat down on the chair indicated.

'Yes, he's the chap,' he replied. 'It was that made me wonder whether there might be a link with the skeleton business, although I shouldn't think it's likely. What it could be is that somebody saw the car going out to Starbarrow Farm last weekend, and after the broadcast this evening thought they'd just let us know without giving themselves away.'

Pollard looked up.

'Interesting that you should say that, Inspector. We met a lady just as we were coming off the moor above Churstow this afternoon. She informed us that one of your chaps who was out there making enquiries about cars using the lane last weekend was wasting his time. He wouldn't get anything out of anybody. Churstow v. The Rest, in fact.'

'She was right enough there,' Inspector Hemsworthy replied with asperity. 'The chap's just got in, with nothing whatever to report. Not a single soul had seen or heard or smelt a car in that lane anytime during the last fortnight for all he could find out. Disgraceful obstruction, that's what it is. But there could quite well be somebody afraid to speak up in front of the neighbours who had some sense of public duty, and who'd phone in without giving a name when there was a chance.'

Pollard considered further.

'How long has the engagement been on?'

'Last Christmas it came out in the *Advertiser*, with both their photos.'

'That's six months ago. You'd think Churstow people,

for instance, would know about it, and hardly think it fishy if young Grant's car made trips out to the farm. And incidentally, the girl was at home last weekend. We had it from her mother this afternoon.'

Inspector Hemsworthy repeated his belief that there was nothing in the phone call. 'Just another nut, most likely,' he said. 'We get plenty of 'em on the line.'

'How did Mr Ling react to the engagement?' Pollard asked, casting round for any further possible explanations.

'I wouldn't know, Mr Pollard. Are you thinking he might be trying to chuck a spanner into the works?'

'It's a possibility, I suppose,' Pollard said doubtfully. 'He's a peculiar bloke. Is there any reason why he might object to Mr Grant personally?'

Here Inspector Hemsworthy was emphatic. Mr Peter Grant was a thoroughly good young chap and popular in the town and round about. Fine tennis player and fond of country life. Nice bit of money left to him by his aunt last year, too. He and his sister each got about £40,000, people said, as well as a half-share in the house, and he was doing well in the firm from all accounts.

'I can't see what more any father could want for a daughter,' he concluded.

They had just decided to take no steps in connection with the anonymous telephone call when the duty sergeant knocked and entered.

'Excuse me, sir,' he said, uncertain to whom he should address himself, 'but there's a party arrived wanting to see Superintendent Pollard about the appeal for information on the telly. They say they saw a young fellow who matched up with the description over at the old lookout Easter Monday last year.'

'They?' Pollard queried. 'How many in the party?'

'Five, sir. A Mr and Mrs Sam Hawkins, their daughter and her boy friend, and a younger lad. 17 Capstick Way's the address. Too many to come in here, so I put 'em in Waiting Room B, pending instructions.'

'Some hope of getting reliable information from a gaggle like that about what they think they saw last Easter Monday twelve month,' Inspector Hemsworthy commented acidly.

40

The sergeant stood his ground.

'It's the chap's hair they're on about.'

Pollard, who had listened with some amusement, looked up with sudden interest.

'Hair?' he asked. 'Do you mean these people say they noticed that he'd had it bleached, but it was beginning to grow out darker?'

'That's what they're saying, sir,' the sergeant replied stolidly. 'From what I could make out it was the girl first spotted it, she being apprenticed to the hairdressing trade, and she pointed it out to the others. Made a joke of it, saying he'd better come along to Crowning Glory in the High Street where she works.'

'Do they strike you as the sort of people who'd come along here with a cock-and-bull story just for a giggle?'

'I wouldn't say so, sir. Hawkins is a superior sort of working-class chap with a job at Letterpress, a local printing works, he says, and his wife seems sensible enough, even if she's a talker. Both in their forties, I reckon.'

'Well,' Pollard said, 'with an age range of about fifteen to forty-five in the party we can soon spot it if they've imagined the whole thing on the strength of the broadcast. Let's go and try them out.'

On going into the waiting room he immediately identified a close-knit matriarchal unit dominated by Mrs Hawkins, an ample woman with permed ginger hair and a briskly competent expression. Her husband, an easy-going type in shirt and trousers, reacted sheepishly on being identified as the leader of the family, and his wife attempted to take over.

'Just a minute, please, Mrs Hawkins,' Pollard interposed. 'Scotland Yard requires full personal particulars from witnesses before statements can be made. My colleague here, Detective-Inspector Toye, will take them.'

As he expected, this created an impression, and while Toye collected the information, he himself was able to observe the family closely. Linda Ethel Hawkins (18), apprentice hairdresser, looked a bright little piece, he thought, not as aggressive as her mother, but very much on the spot. Paul Hoggett (21), Post Office worker, was the solid type. Thomas William Hawkins (14) was so fascinated by his surroundings that he missed out on Toye's request for his full name, and was sharply told by his mother to speak up and not be so daft.

'Now then,' Pollard said, when the operation was concluded, 'let's have a large-scale map, Inspector. I want you to show me exactly where you all were, Mr Hawkins, when you saw a young man on Easter Monday of last year, whom you think was the one described on the News tonight.'

Sam Hawkins located the spot without difficulty. Stoneham was situated on the river Riddon, about three miles from the coast. West of the estuary the land rose steeply to Cattesmoor, and a footpath led up to the top of the spectacular cliffs which formed the coastline for the whole distance to Biddle Bay. The footpath continued for some miles along the cliff top before petering out. After a short distance it passed to the left of a small roofless stone building at a lower level, described on the map as 'Lookout (disused)'. This provided some shelter from the wind, and the Hawkins family had intended to have their picnic lunch there.

'That's all quite clear, thank you, Mr Hawkins,' Pollard told him, returning the map to Toye. 'What time did you arrive at this place?'

'Quarter to one, near enough,' Mrs Hawkins said. 'It's a pull up to get there, and I remember I took a look at me watch half-way, when I stopped to get me breath. Just past the half-hour it was then. I was glad enough when we came in sight of the lookout, feelin' ready for a nice sit-down and me lunch.'

Tommy Hawkins seized his moment.

'I ran on afore the others,' he volunteered in a voice of uncertain pitch, 'an' looked down into the place. Roof's gone, see? An' I saw the bloke in his sleepin' bag, smokin' a fag, with all his clobber chucked around.'

'What did he look like?' Pollard asked.

'Couldn't see much 'cos of the sleepin' bag, only his face, all smothered in hair.'

'What colour was this hair?'

'Darkish. Same as Paul's. But he'd a lot o' mucky yellow hair on his head.'

'You're an observant chap, Tommy,' Pollard congratulated him. 'We'll be seeing you in the Force one of these days. Now, what did all the rest of you notice about this fellow in the lookout?'

Mrs Hawkins was voluble about hippies and layabouts who made a filthy dirty mess of the places where decent people liked to go and enjoy themselves. They'd had to go further along the cliff and climb up on a bank to have their picnic. Then, just as they'd finished eating, they'd seen the hippy come up out of the lookout and start along the path. At this point Pollard cut in deftly.

'I think this must be where you come in, Linda, isn't it?' he asked, and smiled at her.

'Well, being in hairdressing, it was his hair I noticed special,' she said, shyly at first, but gaining confidence as she went on. 'You could see at once he'd had a bleach – a cheap one, I'd say. His hair was in a dreadful state. Then as he went past I could look right down on the top of his head, us being up on the bank, and the bleach'd grown out from the scalp a couple of inches, and the new hair was quite dark like his beard. So I whispered to Paul who was next to me and Mum on the other side, and – and said joking like, that he ought to come along to Crowning Glory where I work.'

'Did you actually see the darker hair next to the man's scalp for yourself, Mr Hoggett?' Pollard asked.

'Yea, I saw it,' Paul Hoggett replied.

'I saw it with my own eyes,' Mrs Hawkins announced, 'and I'll stand up in court any day and say so.'

They were all agreed that the chap had been wearing dirty blue jeans and a brown windcheater, and carrying a rolled-up sleeping bag and bulging rucksack on his back. His height had been much the same as Paul's, five feet six and a half inches. Their estimate of his age ranged from sixteen to twenty-four. He'd walked straight past them without a word, heading towards Biddle Bay, and they'd watched him out of sight a goodish way along, where the path took a dip.

Pollard told the Hawkins family that their information could turn out to be important, and thanked them for coming forward so promptly. It was possible that some of them might be called upon to give evidence in court at a future date. Linda especially might be needed as a witness, and Inspector Toye would type out a brief statement of what she had said, and ask her to sign it, if she agreed with everything in it. Leaving Toye to get on with this job, he started off for their temporary office feeling positively elated. He had no doubt that the youth seen at the lookout on Easter Monday of the previous year had ended up as the skeleton found in Starbarrow kistvaen. However devious the route linking these two points, at least there was now somewhere to start from. In a corridor he unexpectedly ran into the chief constable, and told him of the latest development.

'I seem to remember from the Kittitoe case that you know this area well,' he said, 'so perhaps you can clear up a point that's puzzling me. Even if the chap was sleeping rough, surely he'd have some sort of overnight shelter in mind? He couldn't possibly have made Biddle Bay by dark, starting off so late in the day, and all that north coast of Cattesmoor seems uninhabited moorland on the map.'

'My guess is that he made for the old tin workings,' Henry Landfear replied. 'They're marked on the one-inch map, but you probably thought it just meant shafts and bits of rusty old machinery lying around. Actually there are several stone buildings still standing in various stages of decay. They'd give more protection than the lookout, come to that. That's the sort of thing that gets passed round in footloose circles.'

'How far are they from the lookout?' Pollard asked.

'About eight or nine miles. After that the path gives out, and there's nothing till you get to the farms this side of Biddle. He could have made Biddle the next day all right.

'Farms? They might be worth contacting, perhaps? He could have tried a bit of scrounging. More hopeful than enquiries in Biddle itself after all this time. It would have been full of visitors in Easter week.'

Henry Landfear agreed, and advised a personal call on Superintendent Pratt at the police station.

'He's a very decent chap, and I know he'll do all he can for you at that end. But I agree that it's not promising, unless your bloke got run in, for instance, or was involved in an accident.'

Pollard thanked him and went on his way. When Toye reappeared they spent some time studying large-scale maps of the district. Assuming that the youth seen by the Hawkins family had pushed on towards Biddle Bay, the old tin workings seemed a credible – in fact, the only credible – spot for him to spend the night of Easter Monday. However, after an interval of fourteen months it seemed a waste of time to search for any traces of him there. It was possible, of course, that he had been seen by other walkers, either on the Monday afternoon or on resuming his way towards Biddle Bay. After all, it was a holiday season.

'Most likely he'd meet up with somebody nearer Biddle,' Toye said. 'Look, there's a road out to the farms which must be good enough for cars. It goes a bit further, and then there's a mile or two of footpath marked. People'd take their cars as far as they could, and then park 'em and have a bit of a walk. What about putting out another appeal for information?'

'It's an idea,' Pollard replied, 'but we'd better wait and see if anything more comes in from the first two. We don't want to muddle the public. And of course there are other possibilities. We don't know that the chap didn't think better of it and turn back to Stoneham. And there's another highly suggestive possibility, isn't there? Look at the map. If you cut across the moor roughly south from the tin workings, you land up either at or very near Starbarrow Farm, don't you?'

'You wouldn't expect a chap like that to have a map,' Toye propounded. 'How would he have known where he'd fetch up?'

'The C.C. thinks a certain amount of information about possible pads circulates among the rootless.'

They sat in silence for some moments, visualising a possible arrival at the farm and its outcome.

'Hold it,' Pollard said suddenly. 'What was the date of Easter last year?'

'30 March,' Toye replied, consulting a pocket diary.

'Remember that Ling said the place was unoccupied for a few weeks at the end of March last year?'

They looked at each other.

'If it's true, and it ought to be easy to check up on, could it be that the chap blundered into some funny business? Here, this is the wildest speculation. We've no evidence that he didn't make for Biddle. We'll go over there after breakfast tomorrow and get some enquiries started.' Pollard yawned prodigiously. 'I'm for bed,' he concluded. 'This day seems to have been going on for ever.'

Chapter 4

While dressing on the following morning Pollard wondered how early they could decently descend on Superintendent Pratt at Biddle Bay. It seemed only fair to let the chap deal with his own immediate problems and the morning's mail first. Meanwhile he and Toye could profitably fill in time by finding out the exact dates between which Starbarrow Farm had been unoccupied in the spring of 1975. The journey out there was time-consuming, and it seemed worth trying a phone call to Geoffrey Ling, even if the net result was the slamming down of the receiver at the other end. Anyway, the immediate priority was a decent breakfast, which, if he remembered rightly, you could bank on in this particular pub. Going down to the dining room he saw Toye in a far corner engrossed in the menu, and was immediately intercepted by a posse of newsmen strategically placed near the door.

'Not a syllable,' he told them, 'until I've knocked back what hotel brochures call a full, repeat, full English breakfast.'

Unmoved by their groans and protests he joined Toye, and addressed himself to cereal, bacon and eggs with sausages, tomatoes and mushrooms, toast and marmalade and coffee, while sketching out a proposed course of action.

'Even if we get dates out of Ling,' he said, 'they'll have to be checked. We can probably push that on to the Yard, though.'

An informal press conference followed in the hotel car

46

park. Pollard listened with enjoyment to an account of an attempt to interview Geoffrey Ling at the farm, and then diverted attention to the Hawkins family, the lookout and the disused tin workings. This handout was received enthusiastically and had the desired effect of a rapid dispersal.

'With any luck,' Pollard remarked as he got into the car, 'most of 'em will spend the best part of the day trying to get to the tin workings, weighed down with cameras and wearing town shoes. We'll make for the station, and I'll put a call through to Ling. You can listen in and take notes.'

At the police station they learnt that a report had come in from a man claiming to have seen a youth who corresponded with the broadcast description, in a Stoneham pub on the evening of Easter Sunday, 1975. This report was being further investigated. Several more people had visited the Starbarrow kistvaen recently, and one of these had found it empty on the Friday afternoon of the previous week. This usefully narrowed the time during which the skeleton could have been deposited there.

Pollard's telephone call to Starbarrow Farm was answered promptly by a truculent Geoffrey Ling.

'If you're the Press, then go to hell and stay there,' he was told.

'Superintendent Pollard speaking, Mr Ling,' he replied. 'Good morning. I'm ringing you for further information. What were the actual dates when your house was unoccupied in the spring of last year?'

He sensed at once that the question was unwelcome. There was a pause followed by an abusive outburst.

'I'm not standing for any more bloody police persecution,' Geoffrey Ling shouted.

As he moved the receiver several inches from his ear, Pollard suddenly recalled a remark of the chief constable's.

'Rather an inexact word in the present context,' he commented. 'Not what one would expect from your expertise in making up crosswords.'

'Damn your eyes!' Geoffrey Ling retorted, his tone conveying, however, a hint of gratification. 'Oh, all right, since Britain's become a police state. 20 March to 4 April.'

'Thank you. We shall need confirmation, though. Were you and your wife on holiday?'

A cackle of laughter further lightened the atmosphere.

'On a relict's non-stop larder holiday, say.'

'How many letters?' Pollard asked, making a reassuring gesture in the direction of a startled Toye at the telephone extension, and mentally thanking Providence for recent sessions at *The Times* crossword with Aunt Is.

'Five.'

'What travel firm did you book your cruise with?' he asked.

'Wave Wanderers,' Geoffrey Ling replied, too taken aback for comment.

After this Pollard had little difficulty in extracting the information he wanted. Geoffrey Ling, his wife, and their daughter Kate had driven to London Airport on 20 March, and flown from there to Venice, where they had embarked in the cruise ship *Triton*. On 2 April they returned to London, and spent two nights in an hotel in South Kensington before driving home on 4 April.

Pollard decided to revert to the subject of the empty farm house.

'And during your absence no one was living at Starbarrow Farm, Mr Ling?' he asked, and sensed an immediate return to wariness.

'If they were, it was without my knowledge and consent.'

'Did either you or your wife or daughter notice any sign of 'anyone having been on the premises when you returned?'

'I didn't. If *they* did, they said nothing about it to me.'

'Before you went away, did you arrange for anybody to come out and do jobs? A builder, for instance?'

'I'm not such a bloody fool as to invite people to come messing about on my property. Not that some types wait for an invitation.'

'Can you suggest any caller who may have come uninvited, then?'

'No, I can't,' Geoffrey Ling roared. 'And I'm not answering any more blasted questions, that's flat.' He slammed the receiver down violently.

Pollard pushed the telephone aside and rested his folded

arms on the table.

'Interesting,' he said. 'Why does he get so hot under the collar when any interest's shown in the time when the house was shut up? Obviously he either knows or suspects something offbeat happened in his absence.'

'Can't see him fixing up for somebody to murder our chap while he was safely out of the country, can you?' Toye replied.

'No. Too complicated and dangerous, I should have thought, for anybody who isn't a professional gangster. I suppose he could be one, though. Appearances can be highly deceptive. I wonder what the Yard are unearthing about him? Let's hope they'll get a move on. Could he be shielding someone?'

Their eyes met.

'AQW 227N?' Toye suggested.

'The girl's boy friend,' Pollard said meditatively. 'Then whose was the funny sort of voice? Deep and sort of hoarse. You know, all this is wild speculation, Toye. The job right now is to try to pick up our chap after he left the lookout. We'd better make tracks for the superintendent at Biddle. Why are you looking so put out?'

'That crossword clue Ling had the nerve to try on you. I can't get there. What's a relict?'

'A widow. In this case the old girl whose C-R-U-S-E of oil never ran out when she was making little cakes for Elijah. What shameful ignorance of Holy Writ in someone who's been a churchwarden . . .'

Superintendent Pratt of Biddle Bay was gratified by a visit from Pollard, and anxious to give any help he could. At the same time he held out little hope of an individual youth of hippy type being remembered from among the Easter holiday crowd of 1975.

'There are any number of that sort around these days, Mr Pollard,' he said. 'Unless he made himself conspicuous in some way, I can't see any particular one sticking in people's minds, not after all this time. Still, we'll make a start by looking up our records. Lads like that can get mixed up in all sorts of trouble, as I'm sure I've no need to tell you.'

The records for the period were unproductive. No youth with the physical characteristics of the skeleton found in the Starbarrow kistvaen had fallen foul of the Biddle Bay police. The chief constable's idea of making enquiries at the Cottage Hospital was followed up, but again with a negative result.

'Sleeping rough as he was, it doesn't seem likely that he'd have taken a room here,' Superintendent Pratt said. 'I'll have enquiries made, though, down in what we call the Old Town, where folk aren't too particular who they take in, as long as it's cash down in advance. Sheds out at the back, you see, and old caravans and whatever. The district M.O.H. is always on about it.'

'Suppose our chap came all the way along the cliffs and into Biddle on that side,' Pollard suggested. 'Your C.C. said something about farms that he might have called at on the chance of a job or a handout.'

Superintendent Pratt produced a large scale map.

'There are a couple of farms all right,' he replied, pointing them out. 'Here, on this minor road. It goes on another mile or so, and then fades out into a path which a hiker coming westward would pick up. But I doubt if the sort of chap you're after would hang around the farms. The farmers 've had so much trouble with holidaymakers that they keep pretty fierce dogs, and there are notices warning people off. I'll send one of my men along, though, just on chance, and he can call at the houses on the outskirts of the town, too. I'll ring you at Stoneham if we get on to anything.'

Pollard was suitably grateful for these offers of help, but it was clear that nothing further was to be gained by prolonging his visit. After a short friendly chat he left with Toye, feeling depressed. It was obvious that the chances of picking up the trail of the chap seen at the lookout were extremely poor. And that went for the chance of tracking down a contact between him and some unknown person which might eventually lead to the Starbarrow kistvaen. Of course he might never have come on to Biddle, in which case all the enquiries there were a sheer waste of time. Weighed down by a feeling of frustration, Pollard sat in gloomy silence as Toye waited at the exit from the car park

50

for a chance to edge out into the stream of traffic. Pedestrians hurried past the Rover's bonnet with faintly curious glances at Toye and himself. Suddenly a brisk grey-headed figure with a full shopping basket in each hand came in sight.

With an exclamation Pollard rapidly let the window down further and put out his head.

'Aunt Is!'

'Tom!' Isabel Dennis came up to the car, her face alight with pleasure. 'What incredible luck! I knew you were at Stoneham, of course, but didn't think there was a hope of seeing you . . . And Inspector Toye here too . . . Where are you off to now?'

'Back to Stoneham.'

'Now listen, my dear boy. It's after twelve already. It won't take you any longer to pop up to the cottage for bread and cheese and beer than it would to fight your way into a stuffy crowded bar when you get back. You two go on ahead. The mini's only a couple of minutes from here, and I'll follow on.'

'Sounds all right, don't you think?' Pollard asked Toye, who replied decorously that it would be most enjoyable, and very good of Miss Dennis.

'O.K., then, aunt. Be seeing you. This is great,' he told her.

As they nosed their way out on to the Stoneham road he was surprised to find that his depression had magically lifted, and decided that it must be because of a temporary escape from his case into normal human relationships. For a few moments he indulged in a fantasy of arriving at the cottage and finding Jane and the twins still there.

'No, old son,' he said firmly to Toye as they turned left and began to climb up to Holston, 'you are not, repeat *not*, going to slope off to the pub for your snack. Aunt would be affronted. You and she absolutely clicked that time she gave you breakfast.'

'I remember that breakfast,' Toye said reminiscently. He gave Pollard a quick glance. 'We were properly up against it that time, weren't we?'

'Point taken,' Pollard replied with a grin. 'Funny isn't it, how the job you're on always seems the all-time worst? You must admit this one's a stinker though, and I've got a nasty feeling that we haven't really started to get to grips with it yet . . . Here we are, and I think I hear the mini. I bet Aunt Is knows a short cut out of the town.'

They were soon seated at a table in the kitchen window, enjoying a substantial snack which included homemade bread and tomato chutney, and cans of ice-cold beer from the refrigerator.

'This is super,' Pollard said, munching contentedly. 'Aunt, in spite of your well-known discretion, I suppose you're consumed with curiosity about my skeleton, aren't you?'

'Of course I am,' Isabel Dennis replied. 'I've got a proprietary interest. After all, if you hadn't been staying here, you wouldn't have started off on Possel and got involved, would you?'

'Almost certainly true. Well, I can't see why you shouldn't have a preview of today's evening papers and news on the box. On Easter Monday, 1975, a worthy Stoneham family called Hawkins took a picnic lunch up to the old coastguards' lookout on the cliffs west of the estuary . . .'

Isabel Dennis listened with absorbed attention, at the same time keeping generous supplies of food and drink in circulation. When the narrative came to an end she was silent for a few moments.

'Now let me recap,' she said. 'You've accepted that the Starbarrow skeleton is the skeleton of the man the Hawkins family saw?'

'Yes,' Pollard replied, 'we're prepared to accept that. Anything else would be quite unacceptably fantastic coincidence because of the tie-up with the pathologist's report, wouldn't it, Toye?'

'That's right,' Toye agreed. 'You see, Miss Dennis, it's the business of the hair, and Linda Hawkins being a hairdresser's apprentice that clinches it.'

'So there we are,' Pollard took up, 'and there we're stuck at the moment. The chap emerges from the lookout with his clobber on his back and heads for Biddle, where the chances of picking up his trail seem practically nil.'

His aunt gave him a sharp look.

'He needn't have gone to Biddle at all. If he camped overnight at the old tin workings, which seems a reasonable suggestion, he could perfectly well have headed south from there. If he did, he would probably have gone round Starbarrow and arrived within sight of the farm, as you'll have spotted for yourselves.'

'Yes, we have, actually. But at this point we run into something unexpected and interesting. Starbarrow Farm was unoccupied from 20 March to 4 April. The three Lings were on a Mediterranean cruise. We haven't actually had confirmation from the shipping company yet, but Geoffrey Ling isn't fool enough to lie about a thing like that.'

Isabel Dennis looked taken aback and then gave a wry smile.

'I suppose I've been letting my prejudice against him run away with me,' she admitted.

'Well, let's face it. It's extremely difficult to estimate the time of death accurately over a long period, and it could still be possible that the chap turned up at Starbarrow Farm after the Lings got back, and was murdered then. But if Ling killed him, would he have been crazy enough to flaunt the fact by suddenly dumping the skeleton in the kistvaen over a year later? But let's drop this problem for the moment. I think there are one or two things that you might be able to help us about, Aunt, with all your local knowledge. Had work on the Possel Way started by Easter 1975?'

'No. Heloise Grant died on 20 May – she left the Friends the money they used for it, as I think I told you. The actual work didn't start till the late summer.'

'In the pre-Possel era was there much walking on Cattesmoor?'

'Oh, yes. Local people and visitors often go up there, especially in the summer. You can get up almost anywhere along the Biddle–Stoneham road, although it's very rough and steep in places. The easiest way up is through the villages like Churstow. Or you can go out along the cliffs from both Stoneham and Biddle and cut inland. Here again it's rough and boggy in places, and rather nasty mists

53

come in suddenly from the sea at times.'

'You see what I'm getting at,' Pollard said. 'Suppose our chap did spend the Monday night at the tin workings and then headed south, another bloke could have turned up to meet him at the farm without being in the least noticeable, from what you say.'

'Yes, I think that's fair comment,' Isabel Dennis agreed, 'although, of course, if you do run into other walkers in open country you tend to pass the time of day, don't you?'

'You've got a point there, certainly. Can you suggest anybody who might have been up on the moor on either the Monday or Tuesday of that week?'

'Well, there are quite a lot of local societies besides the Friends with special interests: botany and archaeology and birds and so on. They have their own expeditions but we publish a kind of communal newsletter with all our fixtures in it. I'll get last year's, we can see if any parties were on Cattesmoor then. It's quite possible.'

Pollard looked through the pamphlet with interest.

'The botanists went to an arboretum near Wintlebury on the Monday. £2.20, including tea. Bring your own picnic lunch. I hope they had a good day. Nothing else seems to have been organised for that week. Is Mr G. Akerman, President of the Archaeological Society, the same chap as the Friends' secretary?'

'Yes. Archaeology's his special thing. I suppose he might have been up on Cattesmoor on the Monday having a look at prehistoric monuments like the Starbarrow kistvaen. We have vandal trouble now and again. The wretched creatures managed to pull down a wayside cross last year. But he'd have been working on the Tuesday: he owns the Letterpress printing works in Stoneham.'

Pollard was still studying the pamphlet.

'Mr W. Worth on the General Co-ordinating Committee,' he remarked. 'Well, well. Hardly his line, I should have thought. And Miss D. Grant's on it, too. According to him, she's making an all-out effort to step into her late aunt's shoes as a patron of local activities. What's her brother like?' he asked, skilfully bringing the conversation round to the owner of AQW 227N.

'I've only met him once, at a party at Upway Manor

54

while Heloise Grant was alive. He's an architect, and seemed a nice sensible young man. I expect you know he's engaged to the Ling girl?'

'So I've heard. How on earth did he manage to get to know her? The farm's festooned with threatening notices to would-be callers.'

'They first met on a winter sports holiday. Not last winter, but the one before. They're both outdoor types and good at games. I've heard that Upway Manor is to be divided into two flats, one for them and the other for Davina, but apparently there's a hold-up over planning permission. It's a listed house. Heloise Grant left it to Peter and Davina jointly. They went to live with her about ten years ago, after their parents were drowned in a sailing accident.'

'What a mine of local information you are,' Pollard remarked. 'Well, I suppose we ought to push off, oughtn't we, Toye? This let-up's been super.'

'It's been very good of you indeed, Miss Dennis,' Toye contributed. 'A real pleasure.'

Back on the road again they talked over the facts gathered from Isabel Dennis.

'If Peter Grant and the Ling girl – Kate, isn't she? – first met at winter sports in late '74 or early '75, the affair could have been going ahead by Easter '75,' Pollard argued. 'Was it advanced enough for him to trek out to the farm while the Lings were on their cruise, to water her pet plants, or something? Father needn't have been consulted – probably wasn't. She's a horticulturalist, isn't she?'

Toye thought there was something in the idea, and that it might link up with the anonymous phone call after all. It was generally known now that the chap whose skeleton it was had died in the spring or early summer of 1975, and seeing that the skeleton turned up more or less on the doorstep of Starbarrow Farm, a lot of people would jump to the conclusion that it had been kept there all the time, in a shed or somewhere. Somebody at Churstow, say, might have remembered young Grant's car going out to Starbarrow when the Lings were away, and felt they ought to let the police know.

'I'm coming round to the idea that we ought to see Peter

Grant,' Pollard said, after a pause. 'If he did go out to the place when the Lings weren't there, it's theoretically possible that either he'd already killed our bloke and took the body there to hide, or that they met there, and either murder or manslaughter or justifiable homicide took place, and the body was hidden on the spot. Don't ask me why it was put into the kistvaen to be discovered by the next passer-by fifteen months later: that's a separate issue. But quite apart from the anonymous phone call, I think we ought to take a look at young Grant. I wish I could think of a pretext which wouldn't put the wind up him at this stage, in case he's the killer. Any ideas?'

'One thing did cross my mind,' Toye said, overtaking an articulated lorry with a sudden spurt of speed. 'A B.M.W.'s a pricey affair for a young architect, and it's a recent model. How long has he had it? I mean, did he trade in an older car, after his aunt died and left him a nice bit of cash? And if he did, can we trace it? If he carried a corpse about in it, I suppose there's just the chance there might still be bloodstains or whatever.'

'I'm not sure that your car fixation hasn't got on to something, you know. We can easily find out if and when he changed his car last year, and where the old one is, if he did. The interesting thing will be if the change was after Easter '75, and before his aunt died on 20 May. If it was, I think I'm prepared to tackle him about whether he went out to Starbarrow between 20 March and 4 April, and see how he reacts. And there's this George Akerman who's sold on prehistoric monuments, and keeps an eye on the Cattesmoor ones. I can't imagine that he can be any help to us, but we may as well contact him for good measure. He seems to be an observant type.'

As they approached Stoneham Pollard began to think up a report for his Assistant Commissioner which would justify carrying on the enquiry, at any rate for the present. For some reason the meeting with Aunt Is had cleared off his depression, and he felt that to be taken off the case now would be infuriating. Curiously enough, the only thing that was bothering him at the moment was a niggling feeling that there was something he ought to have asked her about, and hadn't. What it was eluded him. On arrival at the police station he learnt that information had come through from the Yard for him, and the matter vanished from his mind.

Chapter 5

Wave Wanderers, the travel agency, confirmed that the three members of the Ling family had been on a Mediterranean cruise organised by them during the period 20 March to 2 April 1975, and had spent the nights of 2 and 3 April at an hotel in South Kensington as part of the package holiday. Remarking that all this had been a foregone conclusion, Pollard tossed the report over to Toye for the case file, and became immersed in the facts gathered by the Yard about Geoffrey Ling.

'Geoffrey Bruce Ling,' he read. 'Born 1917. Only child of Walter Bruce Ling, actuary. Open scholar of Harminster and Newton College, Cambridge. Placed in First Class of Classical Tripos, Part 1. Offered Oriental Languages in Part 2, and again placed in First Class. Reputation at Cambridge for brilliance and eccentricity. Took no part in university life, was quarrelsome, and settled scores through ruthless practical jokes. Called up for National Service on coming down from Cambridge in summer of 1939. Directed into Intelligence. Developed exceptional ability for deciphering and compiling codes, and continued with this work for the duration of the war and for two further years in post-war Europe. Failed to get the promotion his ability warranted owing to difficult temperament (see above). Returned to England in 1947 and engaged in work on dictionary projects in several languages. Father died in 1948, leaving him financially independent. Bought isolated cottage in East Anglia. In 1950 married Eleanor Pym. One child of the marriage, a daughter, born in 1951. Developed interest in teaching of languages to young children. Taught in several boys' preparatory schools and wrote two successful text books, still widely used in progressive junior schools. In 1970

57

bought remote farm house in Glintshire, and moved there in 1972. Takes no part in local life and is aggressive about his privacy, recently losing a right of way case. Has no police record,' the report concluded, 'but the institution of proceedings against him has been considered on several occasions, in connection with aggressive conduct towards persons alleged to have interfered with what he considers to be his rights.'

Pollard passed the report to Toye, and sat watching him perusing it attentively.

'Hangs together, doesn't it?' Toye said some minutes later. 'The bit about ruthless practical jokes and the skeleton. He must've been hopping mad with the Friends of Cattesmoor over that right of way.'

'All that fits like a glove,' Pollard agreed, 'but it doesn't get us much further. It just confirms that Ling's putting a skeleton into the kistvaen is in character, as we'd already said ourselves. It doesn't suggest that Ling's a homicidal type, and we're still completely stuck with the problem of where the skeleton came from. Let's see what the Yard's unearthed about the Ling females.'

'Eleanor Ling (née Pym),' he read aloud. 'Born 1920; daughter of Harold Pym, owner of wholesale grocery business in Warhampton. Mother died 1922, and Eleanor brought up on farm of father's brother. Educated at country grammar school. Average ability but unacademic. Joined Women's Land Army at outbreak of war and remained in it for the duration. Good reputation as a worker, but described as a placid solitary type and not a good mixer. Father killed in road accident in 1944, leaving her well provided for. On leaving Land Army bought small holding near Cambridge, living alone and taking little part in local life. Married Geoffrey Ling in 1950. One daughter, born 1951. Marriage apparently successful in spite of husband's temperament and unequal intellectual ability. Has developed interest in rural crafts.'

Toye commented that it was wonderful what some women would put up with to get a husband.

'Oh, I expect Ling's tame enough in his home,' Pollard said. 'You need an audience to be a buffoon. It's interesting about those prep schools. I've noticed before that

58

playing to the gallery goes down jolly well with small boys, provided that whoever it is delivers the goods as well, and I'm sure Ling could do that all right. And Ling and his wife do have things in common such as liking seclusion and living in the country. I expect that when he makes an ass of himself it runs off her placid back like water off a duck's. She might draw the line at monkeying about with a skeleton, though . . .'

Kate Ling, born in 1951, had apparently inherited her parents' preference for country life, and to some extent her father's brains. She had taken a first-class degree in horticulture and held a junior lectureship at a horticultural college near Wintlebury. The Yard's report described her as attractive and sociable, adding, as if in surprise, that she appeared attached to her parents and their home. It concluded with her engagement to Peter Grant, architect, of Upway Manor, Stoneham, at the end of 1975.

Pollard found himself reacting personally, suddenly dismayed. Would a time come when people commented with mild surprise that Andrew and Rose appeared attached to their parents? Of course the circumstances were absolutely different, but what about the generation gap? . . . He realised that Toye was looking at him questioningly, and hastily pulled himself together.

'If Kate Ling's fond of her parents,' he said, 'it's reasonable to assume they're fond of her. Let's go back to the possibility that Ling either thinks or knows that Grant went over to Starbarrow while they were all away. I asked him if he, personally, had fixed for anyone to go over and do a job, and he said he hadn't, which is probably true. But he may know that Grant had promised Kate to keep an eye on the garden, for instance. Even if he doesn't suspect his future son-in-law of hiding a corpse on the property, he could be worried that these visits might come out, and lead to Grant being suspected and Kate upset.'

'But if he suspected Grant, surely he wouldn't have chucked the skeleton out on to a public footpath when he eventually found it?' Toye objected.

'He's a hot-tempered impulsive chap,' Pollard said thoughtfully, 'and given to ruthless reactions if he thinks he's being done down. Let's concentrate on timing. He'd been at loggerheads with the Friends over the Possel Way for some time. Then they take him to court about the right of way, and he loses, and has to pay costs as well. This happened on the day we came down to Holston for our holiday: 31 May. The Friends' secretary, this fellow Akerman, rang Aunt Is with the good news just after supper. I remember her saying that Ling was insisting on clearing the route through his property and fencing it himself, and that it would look awful, but save the Friends expense. So it does – look awful, I mean, and the old bastard's made the path so narrow that you get caught up on brambles and things as you go through.' He suddenly broke off and stared at Toye. 'You know,' he went on, 'hacking a way through all that stuff must have been one hell of a job, especially for a chap without much experience of that sort of thing. Not a matter of a couple of hours, and he may have had to get hold of the tools needed. Suppose it took him ten days or so, well into the following week, sweating and cursing the whole time? Say he didn't finish till Thursday, 10 June, the day Mrs Ling went away, and came on the skeleton right at the end? Can't you see him being hit with the idea of scoring off the Friends by getting Possel into the news in the sort of way they'd simply detest?'

'Risky from his point of view, surely?' Toye propounded.

'Well, come to think about it, was it really all that risky? Remember that he'd only been living on the farm for four years. He probably thought the skeleton had been there for ages. He's a literary type, not a scientist, and wouldn't have reacted to its appearance as I did, for instance. If I'm right and something of this sort actually happened, he must have had the shock of his life when the pathologist announced that the thing was only about a year old. And he would have started thinking uncomfortable thoughts about the time when the house was empty in '75.'

Toye sat impassive, his eyes intent with interest behind his owlish horn rims.

'Problem is where he could've found it,' he said at last. 'It wasn't buried. Wouldn't foxes and rats and whatever have pulled the body to bits if it'd just been chucked under a bush?'

Pollard frowned with the effort of visualising the Starbarrow newtake.

'There could be some sort of small building hidden by all the gorse and stuff that's grown up over the years,' he said. 'It's all tangled up, and along the path I remember it was above my head in places, on both sides.'

'How about a search warrant now?' Toye asked.

'We'd be on firmer ground if we knew for sure there was a building of sorts. If only—' Pollard stopped dead and abruptly slammed down his hand on the table. 'I've got it at last! The air photography that Aunt Is said some company with a helicopter did when the work on Possel was starting. It must have been from a low altitude to be any good, and anyway we can have the Starbarrow section blown up. If there's any building there where a stiff could have been stowed away I'm certain we'll be able to spot it. And if Ling refused to let us investigate, we'd get a warrant. You know, I ought to have thought about this air photography before. It's been trying to struggle up out of my subconscious ever since we went to the farm.'

Toye's tenacious mind reverted to Peter Grant.

'What about Grant's car?' he asked.

'Let's see if Crookshank's around,' Pollard replied, getting up. 'He'll know how to get hold of the aerial photograph, and the quickest way of extracting data about Grant's cars from the licensing people. And I've just had another idea. While I'm putting a progress report together for the A.C., you can take the Rover to the garage Grant deals with. Crookshank is sure to know which it is in a smallish town like Stoneham. Say you're not sure the Rover's ticking over properly in some way: you know enough about cars to spin a yarn. Then get the garage hands chatting, and see what you can pick up about Grant's deal when he got the B.M.W.'

Superintendent Crookshank's Mephistophelian eyebrows went up as he listened to Pollard.

'Peter Grant?' he said.

'All very tentative,' Pollard replied. 'At the moment we're working on the theory that somebody parked our chap's corpse at Starbarrow Farm while the Lings were away on their cruise. Peter Grant and Kate Ling had already met at winter sports, and it seems quite reasonable to assume that he'd braved her old man and visited her home. If so, he knew a bit about the geography of the place. Add to this the anonymous phone call giving his car number, and we feel that we've got a possible lead. We think it's worth finding out if he suddenly got rid of his car just then, and acquired his B.M.W.'

'Meaning that there might be giveaway traces of some sort in the old one?'

'Just that. Of course he could quite well have found the chap hanging around the farm and beaten him up a bit too hard, in which case we're wasting time over this car business.'

Crookshank agreed that there was no harm in having a go, but added that he'd be staggered if anything came out of it.

'You can take it as a dead cert that Grant deals with Mayfield's Garage in West Street. It's far and away the best in the whole of this area, and the biggest, too. Ted Callington's the sales manager. He's got the gift of the gab good and proper which ought to help if you can get the chance to pump him. West Street's off High Street, the turning on the right just after Marks and Spencer. Meantime we'll be getting on to the motor licensing department at County Hall, and the firm that did that aerial survey.'

Pollard thanked him, and went off to compile his interim report for the Assistant Commissioner. Toye went out to the car park and sat for some minutes in the driving seat of the Rover, deep in thought. He enjoyed a chance of acting independently but preferred to have a definite plan of campaign before going ahead. Finally he switched on the engine and started off. Five minutes later he drove into the forecourt of Mayfield Garage Limited, noting the gleaming models on display in the show windows and the general air of prosperity. As he entered the spacious interior a number of heads turned, and he realised at once that the Rover had been identified. An obvious foreman detached himself from a trio working on an Austin Cambridge and hurried forward, wiping his hands on a rag. Simultaneously a well-groomed man in his forties with crisp fair hair and an easy manner emerged from a glass-fronted office, and arrived alongside as the car came to a halt.

'The Yard Rover, by Jove!' he exclaimed. 'Lovely job, isn't she? What's the trouble? We're honoured, aren't we, George? I'm Callington, sales manager here.'

Toye got out, introduced himself, and embarked on a description of a slight smell which had led him to suspect a possible leak from the automatic choke. He had tightened a screw, but felt it was advisable to get an expert to have a look.

'Run 'er over into that bay, sir,' the foreman said, 'and we'll do a check right away.'

Toye complied. As he got out of the car again the foreman vanished under the bonnet and became incommunicado. Finding the sales manager at his elbow Toye had no difficulty in getting a conversation going. A favourable comment on the garage's layout and equipment launched Ted Callington on an account of the ever-increasing volume of business handled by the Mayfield, in spite of dicey deliveries of new cars and the difficulties of getting skilled mechanics.

'Everybody's saying money's tight,' he said, 'but round here people are buying cars all right.'

'Not only in the lower price range from what's on the road,' Toye commented. 'I've seen a B.M.W. I could do with. Red. Looks a treat.'

'That'll be Mr Grant's,' Ted Callington replied enthusiastically. 'Sold it to him last year, as soon as we'd got it into the window. First delivery after the Easter holiday, on the Wednesday it was. The boss wondered if we'd get stuck with her, seeing she was a bit pricey, but I said let's take delivery now for God's sake as we've got the chance. It boosts a garage to have cars in that class on show.'

'Mr Grant must be a warm bloke,' Toye observed with a suitable note of envy. 'Successful businessman, I suppose?'

'He's quite a youngster, actually. Young architect in a local firm. His aunt put up the money – most of it, anyway. He traded in his Morris Marina. She was Miss Grant of Upway Manor, and what you call a local figure. She left over £100,000: fell off a ladder and broke her neck a month after buying her nevvy the B.M.W.'

'I could do with the sort of aunt who'd buy me a B.M.W. out of a display window as though it was a push bike.'

'Couldn't we all? She'd promised him a new car for his birthday and told him to look round for something he liked. He'd been havering a bit and didn't seem able to make up his mind, but the minute he set eyes on the B.M.W. he went for it flat out. It was partly she was bucked at his being made a partner in his firm so soon, he told me, that she agreed to cough up for it.'

At this point Toye was requested to rev up the engine and the conversation was broken off. He engaged in a reassuring discussion with the foreman, George Fry, who had further tightened a screw, and finally managed to extricate himself, feeling that he had contrived to learn all that Ted Callington could usefully tell him.

Back at the police station he found Pollard reading over his report on the case for the Assistant Commissioner with a dubious expression.

'I only hope this'll keep the boss quiet pro tem,' he said, putting it down. 'Well? Had any luck?'

'It went my way all right,' Toye told him. 'Callington came breezing up the minute I drove into the place, and you didn't need to try to get him talking. I said something about noticing Grant's B.M.W., and he was off. He said Grant bought it the day they put it in the show window, the Wednesday after Easter, trading in a Morris Marina, and his aunt footing the rest of the bill. But Grant had been thinking of getting a new car for some time, Callington said . . .'

'Interesting but inconclusive,' Pollard commented when Toye's narrative came to an end. 'Can't you see Counsel for the Prosecution and Counsel for the Defence both turning it to account in court? I wonder what the chances are of getting hold of Grant this evening?'

The sudden appearance of Superintendent Crookshank put an end to the discussion.

'We've had a bit of luck which'll save time,' he announced. 'Inspector Hemsworthy remembered that he'd seen those aerial photographs you were talking about, Mr

Pollard, pinned up round one of the rooms at the Museum. The company that took 'em presented a set. The Museum's just for stuff of local interest, and it's run by volunteers mostly. Miss Grant who was taking that walk you met up with happened to be on duty, and seeing she was there when the skeleton was found, she understood the section you'd be wanting.'

He handed Pollard a cardboard tube. It contained a section of a photograph about four feet long and a foot wide. Toye cleared the table, and they spread out the photograph and weighted down its two ends. As Pollard had expected, it had been taken from a low altitude and showed the area in remarkably clear detail. He looked down at it, momentarily fascinated by this godlike view of a landscape through which he had progressed slowly and insignificantly at ground level, with not much more perception than an insect's of his surroundings as a whole. There were the buildings of Starbarrow Farm, the original long house and the subsequent additions. There, too, tiny but distinct, was the kistvaen, where his involvement in this deeply puzzling case had begun so unexpectedly ... He surfaced abruptly as a constable brought in a powerful electric lamp and proceeded to plug it into a socket. As Toye returned to the table with a lens, Superintendent Crookshank, who had been poring over the photograph, suddenly jabbed at it with his forefinger.

'Looks to me that something's sticking out behind a sort of thicket just here,' he said.

'You're dead right,' Pollard agreed a minute later after a scrutiny with the lens. 'It's not a building though. It's a flat surface with biggish stones on it. What's the betting that it's a well-head? Must be a disused well.'

After another inspection Crookshank became almost animated.

'That'll be it,' he said. 'When they sank a shaft for the one the Lings use now, they'll have chucked a lot of rock and stuff down the old one to fill it up. Then last year somebody bunged your chap in and put the top on again. It looks like a great flat bit of wood or metal to me. If you find the missing bones belonging to the skeleton down there, you're home and dry.'

'Not quite home,' Pollard replied. 'Remember Ding, dong, bell? The lad who chucked poor pussy in wasn't the one that yanked her out again, was he? Look here, we want to be absolutely sure of our facts before we weigh in with a search warrant. Who owned Starbarrow Farm before the Lings?'

Crookshank scowled as he struggled in vain to remember.

'Blessed if I can call the bloke's name to mind,' he said. 'The agents were North and Searle, though. I know Bob Searle, and he used to say it looked as if they'd got it round their necks for keeps. It stood empty for four or five years. I'll give him a ring at his place. The office'll be shut by now. Do you want that lamp any more? All right, Jones. Bring it along.'

In his absence Toye expressed admiration.

'Spot on, that air photograph, sir.'

'A bit late in the day,' Pollard replied. 'If I'd only thought of it before, we'd have saved valuable time. The real luck was that Aunt Is happened to mention it. But we're not going to stick out our necks until we've got this well-head affair identified, all the same.'

Superintendent Crookshank returned well-primed with information. The vendor of Starbarrow Farm had been a Mr Danby Blake, a so-called gentleman farmer who had lost a packet over it and been obliged to sell up in 1965. He had come in from up the country somewhere, quite sure that with modern methods he could make a success of Starbarrow, whatever the local farmers said. He tried a lot of ambitious schemes and came to grief as everybody said he would. He was now working for a salary on Lord Landgrove's home farm at Deepacres Park, near Winnage.

'I think we'll pop over and call on him presently,' Pollard said. 'I expect he had big ideas about the water supply, among other things. See if he's on the phone, Toye. Super, we're grateful to you for all this help, you know.'

Crookshank expressed gratification in a characteristically offhand manner, and took his departure as Toye handed the telephone receiver to Pollard. Mr Danby Blake sounded mystified, but was ready to give any information he could about Starbarrow Farm.

'Not that I ever want to hear the bloody place mentioned again,' he added, 'seeing that I all but went bust over it. But come along by all means and have a drink tonight. We're the first house on the right, about five hundred yards beyond the Deepacres main gates if you're coming towards Winnage.'

After writing up their notes on the day's developments they went back to their hotel, where Pollard rang Jane. Against a distant background of small piping voices they talked in their usual motoring code about his activities, and he told her of the confusing network of local byways in the area.

'Aunt Is sent love and everything to you and the brats,' he told her, after describing the snack lunch at the cottage. 'How are they?'

'Fighting fit. Like a word with them?'

He gathered that the in-thing was now practising for the school sports, but the garden was a bit small for it. When he came home would he take them up to the Common? He promised, had a final word with Jane, and rang off. At least the generation gap wasn't making itself felt yet, he reflected, heading for the hotel dining room.

Danby Blake, fortyish and suntanned, received Pollard and Toye hospitably, introduced his wife, and offered drinks. They both appeared philosophical about their changed fortunes.

'I can't say we're wildly thrilled at living in a three-bedroomed house bang on the road,' he said, indicating his surroundings with a sweeping gesture. 'All the same, there's a lot to be said for a definite job with fixed hours and a regular monthly cheque. Not to mention letting someone else do all the worrying. And Lord Landgrove's jolly decent to us, isn't he, Nan?'

Mrs Blake, an outdoor type of about her husband's age, agreed.

'Starbarrow was super,' she said. 'Living out there was heaven in some ways. You felt as if you owned the earth. But Dan's had marvellous luck to land this job. And I don't mind admitting that the house was hell to run! We couldn't afford to modernise it properly, and any help just wasn't on, of course. I don't know myself with all the mod

67

cons here. I must push off now if you'll excuse me: cake-making for the village fête tomorrow.'

'Well,' Danby Blake said, when Toye had closed the door behind her and returned to his chair, 'it's this skeleton stunt, I suppose? Ling's three-quarters of the way round the bend, of course, but I shouldn't have thought he'd actually murder anybody. What can I tell you about the place?'

'What's the water supply like?' Pollard asked.

Danby Blake grimaced.

'That's a sore spot. It was water supply that bowled us out in the end. We bought the place in '58, having been assured that the house well and the small stream through the fields on the south side never ran dry. In the summer of '59 they both did, and I had to spend the earth on deepening the house well and putting storage tanks into the fields. After that we got on a bit better, and I planned to clear and improve the newtake – that's the enclosed area behind the house. I called in water engineers about deepening the old well, and they said it was a near cert, but after they'd put down a twelve foot trial bore without hitting a decent inflow of water, funds ran out, and I had to call it off. I—'

'What did you do about this old well? Wasn't it a possible danger to straying stock?'

'I had all the stuff chucked back and the timber they'd used, and whatever, and we put a dirty great sheet of iron over the hole and weighted it down with chunks of rock.' Danby Blake broke off and eyed Pollard suspiciously. 'Look here, if Ling's been fool enough to shift the cover and somebody fell in, it's his responsibility, not mine. Anyway, the shaft was filled up almost to the top. You couldn't have killed yourself, even if you did fall in.'

'Thank you,' Pollard said, 'that's very helpful information. Would it have been possible for a chap on his own to shift the chunks of rock and the sheet iron?'

Danby Blake's eyes widened.

'If he was a reasonably hefty bloke, yes,' he replied after a moment's consideration. 'Of course it would have sunk into the ground a bit after all this time, and got partly overgrown round the edges, I should think.'

'Here's an aerial photograph of the farm,' Pollard said.

'Would you mark the position of the well-shaft as accurately as you can?'

Danby Blake switched on a reading lamp and bent over the photograph.

'It was just about here,' he said. 'Quite near the house ... I'm not sure you can't see a bit of the sheet iron. Amazing what detail comes out in those things.' He handed back the photograph with a wry grin, remarking that in spite of everything it made him feel a bit nostalgic.

Pollard and Toye left shortly afterwards for Stoneham.

'Keep your eyes skinned for a call box,' Pollard said. 'I'm going to ask for Boyce and Strickland to come down overnight.'

'Meaning that you're getting a warrant and opening up this dud well tomorrow?'

'This is it. We've got to have proper photographic records, and with any luck we'll find the missing bones. It's definitely a job for the boys.'

They stopped in the next village for Pollard to put through the call. Back in Stoneham he took the necessary steps to get a search warrant. It was late when at long last they reached their hotel. Pollard stifled a gigantic yawn.

' "And the morning and the evening were the second day," ' he quoted. 'I can't believe it. We seem to have been here for weeks.'

Toye, a churchman with an evangelical bias, looked momentarily askance, but agreed that he felt that way himself.

Chapter 6

Detective-Sergeants Boyce and Strickland, the photographic and finger-print experts of Pollard's team, arrived by car in time for breakfast the next morning. In the course of the meal Pollard briefed them on the case and the job ahead.

'That'll be a new one on us, sir,' Strickland said. 'First time we've done a well for clues.'

'Lucky there's not much water in it,' Boyce remarked. 'We've left our skin-diving outfits behind.'

'It certainly isn't dry,' Pollard said, anticipating censure from Toye on this levity. 'Some water must seep in, judging from deposits on the skeleton, but it won't interfere with the job. The thing is that you chaps have got to go to work like the archaeological blokes who shift soil with teaspoons. We want the missing bones, and some of 'em are damned small. Bash about, and we'll never find 'em. I'm assuming for the moment that the skeleton came from the well,' he added cautiously.

'O.K., sir,' Boyce and Strickland assured him, and exchanged brief winks.

'Well, let's get moving then. One of you had better collect some sandwiches. It could be a long job, and I don't see Ling laying on lunch for us, do you, Toye?'

'I'd be surprised,' Toye replied seriously.

A small heap of official-looking mail was waiting for Pollard at the police station. Impatient to be off, he glanced quickly through the letters and passed them to Toye for filing. It was not until he picked up the last one that he stopped short of tearing it open, and stood staring at the featureless block capitals on a manila business envelope.

'Look at this effort,' he said. 'Over to you Strickland. There might be a useful dab under the flap.'

The envelope was carefully slit and its contents, a folded half-sheet of typing paper, shaken on to the table and opened out with forceps. Its message was in block capitals similar to those on the envelope:

'ASK PETER GRANT WHY HE WAS UP HALF THE NIGHT IN THE GARAGE AT UPWAY MANOR CLEANING HIS CAR INSIDE AND OUT ON 1 APRIL 1975.'

'Hoax?' queried Toye. 'A sort of April Fool?'

Pollard looked up from checking the date in his diary's calendar for 1975.

'According to that sales manager bloke you talked to, Grant bought his B.M.W. on 2 April at the drop of a hat, after havering about getting a new car for some time. For some reason he suddenly made up his mind, and cleaned up his Morris Marina ready to trade in on the night of 1

April. Of course, this mayn't mean a thing as far as we're concerned. After all, you've got to make up your mind sometime about changing your car. But this letter coming on top of that phone call shows that somebody's interested in Grant's doings, and has been for the last fifteen months anyway.'

Toye asked if you could see into the garage from the road.

'Yes, you can. If you stand at the gates it's down a short length of drive and straight in front of you. But the house isn't on a road that leads anywhere, except up on to Cattesmoor. There aren't likely to have been casual passers-by, I mean. Possibly moor walkers, I suppose, but hardly after dark in early April.'

'What did the household consist of in April '75?'

'That's something we'll have to look into when we're through with this well job ... Got anything up, Strickland?'

'Smudged glove prints on the letter and the envelope, sir, and what look like men's prints from handling the envelope.'

'Well, we'll leave it pro tem and push off.'

The two police cars set out in convoy, Pollard and Toye leading in the Rover. After several weeks of unbroken sunshine the sky was heavily overcast, and there was a hint of thunder in the still air. When they came out on to Cattesmoor from the land leading up from Churstow, they entered a vast, empty and vaguely sinister world.

'It's enough to give you the willies up here this morning,' Toye remarked unexpectedly as he drove with extreme care over the rough surface.

'Hankering after the bright lights?' Pollard asked with a grin. 'It's not the moor that's giving me the willies,' he went on, 'it's the case. As I've said before, I've got a nasty feeling that we're still only scratching about on the surface. Even if we find unshakeable evidence that the hippy from the lookout turned into the skeleton in the kistvaen during a sojourn in the well we're going to investigate, are we any further on? How did the hippy die, and who concealed his body? Here, let's have the binoculars. The farm's just coming in sight.'

A couple of minutes later he reported that nobody seemed to be around but windows were open, so that at least the family had not gone off on another cruise. Fifty yards short of the farm he told Toye to stop, and Boyce and Strickland drew up behind them.

'We don't want to look like an assault group,' he said. 'I'll go ahead with the warrant. Come on when I sign to you.'

There was still no sign of life as he reached the garden gate, but the click of the latch started up a torrent of hysterical barking inside the house. The door opened, the black and white spaniel shot out and slobbered wildly over his shoes, and he was confronted by Mrs Ling in a service-able nylon overall. She looked at him with a kind of grave detachment, and he knew at once that she realised what he had come for ... I bet it isn't the first time her crackpot husband has landed himself in one hell of a mess, he thought. She's hardened to it ...

'Good morning, Mrs Ling,' he said. 'May I have a word with your husband, please?'

Before she could answer Geoffrey Ling appeared at a bedroom window. Resting his arms on the sill he surveyed Pollard with an air of reckless amusement.

'What can I do for you, Superintendent?' he enquired with mock politeness.

'Nothing, Mr Ling, at the moment,' Pollard replied. 'I have called to tell you that, acting on information received, we are going to open up the unused well in your newtake.'

There was a short pause. Pollard realised that Mrs Ling was signing herself off by shutting the front door.

'Well, who's stopping you?' Geoffrey Ling demanded.

'As the representative of the law I'm unstoppable, Mr Ling. Do you wish to see the search warrant I have with me?'

'No.' As he uttered the monosyllable Geoffrey Ling vanished from sight with the abruptness of a pantomime clown disappearing down a trap door. Pollard turned and walked towards the gate.

'What on earth goes on?'

He glanced round to see an extremely pretty girl at another first-floor window. She had apparently just got out of bed, and on seeing him grabbed ineffectively at the shoulder straps of her nightdress. He hurried out of the garden without engaging in conversation, and returned to his support, to find Boyce and Strickland lamenting the fact that they had no binoculars with them.

'Past the farmhouse and then bear right to the newtake,' he told Toye.

They skirted the farm buildings, parked the two cars among the trees of the windbreak, and entered the newtake at the western end of the right of way. Access had been provided by the simple expedient of knocking down a small section of the encircling drystone wall. Similar rough and ready methods of clearing the track had been used. Gorse and bramble bushes, bracken, and the occasional dwarf rowan tree had been savagely lopped, and the debris flung on either side and left to wither.

'The well's on the house side, not far from where you come out again on to the public path,' Pollard said, striding ahead. 'There it is, behind this thicket.'

They squeezed through the two strands of wire forming part of Geoffrey Ling's very amateur attempt at fencing, and stood looking down at a piece of heavy sheet iron under a pile of stones. Jackets were peeled off in an eloquent silence.

'Hold on,' Pollard said, pausing when half out of his. 'We'll have a photograph, Boyce, before we shift this little lot.'

In due course the stones, some of them sizeable, were removed and stacked, and the unwieldy sheet iron heaved up and dragged to one side. Immediately a revolting smell rose from the well shaft, which Danby Blake had apparently used as a rubbish dump after abandoning the idea of extending it down to the permanent water table.

'Phew!' Boyce commented, holding his nose before embarking on further photography.

The other three watched him, perspiring in the sultry heat and hitting out at the swarm of flies attracted by the stench.

'For God's sake smoke, Strickland,' Pollard said. 'I wish I hadn't given it up. Now then, Toye, let's have a look.'

The bricks lining the shaft were streaked with green

73

slime where surface moisture had seeped in and trickled down, and some of them had fallen inwards where the mortar had crumbled away. A jumble of rusty tins, ends of rope and discarded household effects reached to within a few feet of the top, and a zinc tub, tilted to one side, was partly full of nauseous looking dark liquid.

'Maggots!' Toye exclaimed triumphantly.

'We've got to get that tub thing out without spilling the muck inside it,' Pollard said with sudden decision. 'I wonder if all this junk goes down to the bottom and it's safe to step on it?'

With an improvised rope round him as a precautionary measure, Toye, the smallest and lightest of the team, lowered himself into the shaft and succeeded in getting the tub level. He attached ropes to the handles, and steadied it as Boyce and Strickland hoisted it up. Pollard took a sample of the liquid in a sterilised bottle, and the rest was slowly and carefully poured off. In the residual mud were three small bones.

'Metacarpals, or metatarsals,' he said with a grin. 'Don't ask me which.'

In a jubilant atmosphere Toye suggested going down again for another look round.

'Cuh!' Boyce broke in. 'Here's that girl!'

Pollard looked up and saw a slim figure in blue jeans advancing from the direction of the house. As he went forward to meet her, the girl stopped.

'Can I talk to whoever's in charge, please?' she called to him.

'Good morning,' he said, coming up to her. 'I'm Detective-Superintendent Pollard. You're Miss Ling, aren't you?'

'Yes, I'm Kate Ling,' she replied. 'I want to talk to you. Let's go into the barn. It's cooler in there.'

They walked in silence towards a stone building with an Early English arch over the doorway.

'Is this part of the pilgrims' chapel?' he asked.

'Quite right,' she said. 'There are a couple of filled-in windows of the same period on the other side. I'd like to restore it now that the Possel Way's been opened up, but it wouldn't be the slightest use suggesting it to Father, of course ... Do you mind sitting on these tea chests?'

They sat down facing each other. At close range Kate Ling was even better to look at, Pollard thought, wondering how Geoffrey Ling could have fathered anything so attractive. In essentials her face was her mother's with the same good brow and regular features, though without the heaviness of the older woman. Instead it was vitalised by her father's vivid blue eyes and a strong hint of his intelligence and dynamic quality. She suddenly broke the silence.

'It's the men in my life, as the women's magazines would say,' she told him. 'They're simply driving me up the wall. Take Father, to start with. You see, he's always been like this. Doing quite crazy things to annoy people who've annoyed him, I mean. He can't adjust to a situation. Mother can, of course, or she'd never have survived – oh dear, I'm not doing this a bit well! I know the police don't answer questions, so we'd better take a hypothetical case ... Suppose a man found a human skeleton in his garden, and put it into a public place for a joke. If it's proved that he did, or if he – well, saw the writing on the wall and owned up, what would happen to him?'

'He might face a charge of failing to report a discovery of human remains to the police,' Pollard replied noncommittally. 'If he had tried to mislead the police in any way it could be a serious matter.'

'Would he be sent to prison?'

'That would depend on circumstances.'

There was a pause during which he waited for Kate Ling to voice a further anxiety.

'Of course nobody who'd – who'd killed someone would throw out the skeleton ages afterwards, almost on their own doorstep,' she said, a shade defiantly. 'Not unless they were certifiable, anyway.'

'It would hardly be the sort of thing anyone *compos mentis* would do,' he agreed, and sensed her relief.

'Well then, there's Peter Grant, my fiancé,' she went on. 'It's about him that I'm so frightfully worried. You may have found out already that he came out here while we were away on a cruise at Easter last year. Mother and I didn't tell Father, but we both thought it was a good idea for somebody to keep an eye on the place, and I did want the roses watered if there wasn't much rain. It's been a job getting a garden going . . .'

'Miss Ling, just exactly why is this bothering you so much?' Pollard pressed.

'You must know perfectly well,' she said impatiently. 'It's clear as daylight from the papers that the hippy, this skeleton in the kistvaen, according to the police, vanished into thin air just about then. And Peter's getting beastly anonymous letters. He told me about the first one last night, and now he's rung to say there's been another. Perhaps the police are getting them too, from someone who's trying to make out he's a murderer. People seem to be laying off Father now, and concentrating on Peter. I suppose it's sunk in that Father wasn't here.'

'What are these anonymous letters about?' Pollard asked.

'About coming out here, and changing his old car for the B.M.W. just then. As if – well, you can see the idea.'

'That he might have brought a corpse out here and hidden it, and thought there could be traces in the old car?'

Kate nodded without speaking.

'You know, much the best thing for Mr Grant would be to bring those letters along to us,' Pollard told her.

'I *know*,' she said, beating with her fists on her knees. 'I keep telling him so! He's hopeless. He's got a thing about dragging us into it. He'll be furious, but I'm going to tell him that I've talked to you about it all, and he can damn well hit the roof. He's taking me to a dance tonight, and I'll *make* him listen.'

Pollard wrote down the telephone number of the police station at Stoneham and gave it to her.

'Either of you can ask to be put through to me at any time,' he said, 'or just leave a number for me to ring if I'm out. And going back to the first of your worries, anyone who had carried out the sort of practical joke we were talking about would be wiser to let the police know about it, as things have turned out.

'*Men*,' she said, with a wealth of expression, getting to her feet. 'Not you: you've been great. Thanks a lot.'

She touched him lightly on the shoulder and was gone.

Pollard sat on for a couple of minutes deep in thought. Finally he emerged from the agreeable coolness of the old barn to find the rest of his team reclining under the trees, and heard that Strickland had clinched matters by finding a long bleached hair, dark near the roots and caught on a bit of wood.

By teatime the various finds from the well-shaft had been handed over to the pathologist who had examined the skeleton, and Boyce and Strickland had departed for London. Over cups of tea Pollard gave Toye details of his conversation with Kate Ling.

'As far as Geoffrey Ling and Peter Grant go,' he said, 'we'll let things simmer for the next twenty-four hours. I've got a hunch that there'll be developments, anyway where Ling's concerned. In the meantime there are a couple of leads worth following up. One's finding out who was living in Upway Manor at the beginning of April last year. On the face of it the most likely person to have spotted Grant cleaning his car that night would be someone in the house. His sister, for instance, although it's difficult to imagine what motive she could have for getting him convicted for murder or manslaughter. Not money: Hemsworthy said they each got about £40,000 and a half-share in the house from the aunt last year. Young Grant's taking Kate Ling to a dance tonight; and incidentally, if he's expecting a pleasant evening, he's got another think coming. She may be besotted about him, but she's a forceful and forthright young woman. I'll go along to Upway Manor and register surprise that he isn't at home. With any luck it'll lead to a cosy chat with Davina Grant to renew old acquaintance: I think it's better for me to go alone. Less official, and easier to pump her. You take a break and go to the flicks if there's anything on you can sit through.'

Toye was doubtful, but said he would shop around. He asked Pollard what other lead he had in mind.

'We've got to put in some more work on picking up our bloke's trail after the Hawkinses lost sight of him on the cliffs. We can take it as read now that he left Starbarrow Farm as a skeleton sometime during last weekend. What we've got to find out is when and how he got there, either alive and kicking, or as a corpse. You remember this George Akerman who goes around vetting the antiquities on Cattesmoor? Well, there's just the chance that he may have spotted a hippy type sleeping rough during the week after Easter. Worth asking him, anyway. But we'll leave him till tomorrow. I want to concentrate on Davina Grant tonight.'

After they had written up their notes Toye went off to investigate the programmes of Stoneham's cinemas. Pollard sat on for a time meditating, occasionally referring to the file. In spite of the progress made during the day he still had the frustrating feeling of merely skating about on the surface of his case. What, he asked himself, was behind the anonymous attempts to cast suspicion on Peter Grant? Were they being made by the killer of the hippy, who must in that case also have it in for Grant? Or was Grant the killer himself, and the author of the phone call and the letters in an attempt to confuse the trail? Pollard found himself wanting to reject this possibility for Kate Ling's sake, but of course it called for the fullest investigation. He would leave a note at Upway Manor that evening, requesting in official language Grant's presence at the police station on the following morning. Having decided on this move and written the note, he debated the line he should take with Davina Grant in his attempt to get information on the members of the household in April 1975. In the end he decided to play it by ear, and left the police station for his hotel and a call to Jane.

It seemed probable that Peter Grant would be taking Kate Ling out to a meal before the dance, but Pollard dallied over his steak and chips to avoid all risk of finding him at Upway Manor. It was eight o'clock when he set out on foot. The clouds had dispersed, and it was a sunny warm evening.

Pilgrim Lane was almost deserted at this hour, and Pollard concluded that most of its residents must be having a Saturday evening out. A small group of youths in crash helmets and leather jackets stood round a Honda parked at the kerbside in earnest confabulation. An old man in shirtsleeves with a scraggy neck looked down at him from an upper window, contentedly smoking a pipe, a budgerigar's cage hung out to catch the last of the evening sun. A grubby small child looked up at him from a doorstep as he passed, but otherwise he met no one. The street seemed shorter than he remembered it, and he was soon beyond the builder's yard and the modern bungalows, and at the point where Upway Manor was just visible in the trees, halfway up the hill ahead. It was just about here, Pollard thought, that the B.M.W. had passed him, coming back into Stoneham. A short distance farther on he came to the first Possel Way signpost, and the road began to rise steeply. He came to a halt on the Stoneham side of the Manor gates, and stood listening intently. A few steps further enabled him to look down the straight drive into the garage. Its doors were open, and as before there was only one car, an Austin Cambridge as far as he could see. He bore left and prospected, and was relieved to see that the B.M.W. was not drawn up at the front door. There was a light in one of the ground-floor rooms, but no one was visible through its open windows.

Acting on a sudden impulse Pollard approached the house noiselessly, walking on the edge of the lawn. He noted that the slightly neglected appearance of the garden which had struck him on his first visit was now more marked. As he drew nearer to the windows he heard a curious sound coming from the room. After a second or two he identified it as something like tough paper being cut vigorously with a large pair of scissors. It stopped suddenly, and a shadow fell on one of the windows. He instantly stepped off the grass and crossed the gravel sweep in front of the house with deliberately firm tread. As he rang the front door bell deep barking and growling came from inside the hall. The next moment Davina Grant's head appeared through the nearer window.

'Good evening, Miss Grant,' he said. 'It's Superintendent Pollard. I hope I'm not disturbing you '

In the gathering dusk it was difficult to see her expression clearly, but he sensed sudden expectation followed by disappointment, and also some embarrassment. She regained her self-possession swiftly, however.

'Superintendent Pollard!' she exclaimed. 'Why, what a surprise! Wait just a minute and I'll let you in.'

Rather a long moment, he thought, listening to sounds of hurried movement inside the room. Then he could hear the dog being reassured, and a bolt shot back. The front door opened to reveal Davina Grant holding a golden labrador by the collar.

'Won't you come in?' she said rather breathlessly. 'Don't mind Rex. He's not in the least savage once he sees we know people.'

Pollard tactfully admired the labrador, remarking that it was good sense to have a guard dog in an isolated country house.

'And what a lovely house it is, Miss Grant,' he added, looking round the panelled hall and at the elegant curve of the staircase.

She gave him an arch little glance.

'Well, we think so, you know. Actually it's listed Grade Two. Not that we bother about that sort of thing, but when your family's lived in a house for over two hundred years, you begin to feel part of it somehow. But do come into the drawing room.'

Amused by the Edwardian designation he followed, and got an instant impression of a beautiful room, also panelled, and with graceful alcoves on either side of the fireplace housing displays of china. He saw that an upright chair had been thrust back from a bureau piled untidily with papers. Beside it was an overflowing wastepaper basket. There were portraits, presumably of past generations of Grants, on the walls, and some fine pieces of period furniture about the room, but also a rather surprising amount of miscellaneous litter.

'Do sit down.' Davina Grant indicated an armchair, and sank into another facing it. 'How nice to meet again, isn't it? I do apologise for all this mess in the room, but it's the Summer Fête of the Friends of Cattesmoor in a fortnight, and I'm simply *submerged*. It's always held in our grounds, you see. Naturally I'm carrying on the tradition.'

'The late Miss Heloise Grant was a prominent figure in the neighbourhood, I gather?' Pollard asked.

'Oh, yes. She was involved in endless things: the Bench, Church affairs, the W.I., the Museum and so on. And very much with the work of the Friends of Cattesmoor. She left

80

the money for the opening up of the Possel Way, you know. It's all left me with such a lot of responsibilities. It's so fortunate that the Friends have a simply *wonderful* secretary in George Akerman – I mentioned him before, I think. I really don't know how I should have coped with the Fête without his help. I shall certainly try to simplify things next year, but we both felt it would be more tactful to leave the organisation unchanged this year, as it's my first in charge . . .'

As she talked on, flushed and bright-eyed, Pollard observed her with interest. Her pose was ungainly as she sat leaning forward with hands gripping one knee, and suggested determination and tension, he thought. And unless I'm very much out she's in love with this Akerman chap, and for a moment thought he'd turned up unexpectedly when I arrived at the door just now . . .

He took advantage of a brief pause to ask if the portrait in front of them was the late Miss Grant. The change of subject was obviously uncongenial.

'Yes, it is,' Davina replied briefly. 'It was done when she was much younger, of course.'

Hardly the portrait of a young woman, Pollard reflected. The face was squarish and strong, with shrewd eyes and a humorous mouth, but somewhat lacking in sensitivity. Apparently Davina did not take after the Grant side of her family.

'Well, I mustn't waste your time when you have so much on hand,' he said, as she remained silent. 'It was really your brother I hoped to see. There is a small matter where we think his help might be useful.'

He watched her as he spoke, and saw a sudden sharp focusing of her attention.

'He's out at a dance, and won't be back until late. Can I give him a message?'

'I'll just scribble a note on one of my cards, asking him to look in at the police station in the morning,' Pollard said.

As he wrote he was aware of her satisfaction.

'I'll make sure he gets it. I'll put it out on the hall table, so that he'll see it when he gets in. And now you simply *must* let me give you a drink or some coffee. It's quite a way out here from the town. Did you leave your car up at the gates?'

'I walked out. It's a lovely evening, and I wanted some exercise.'

'Walked!' Davina exclaimed with exaggerated amazement. 'But of course you really are a walker, aren't you? Why, we might never have met otherwise.'

She was on her feet, looking down at him with a provocative teasing expression. He rose politely.

'No, I don't suppose we should,' he agreed prosaically. 'Thank you, a cup of coffee would be very acceptable.'

She turned and went out of the room, followed, to Pollard's relief, by the labrador. Making a grimace he moved quickly and silently over to the wastepaper basket.

At the top, and spilling over on to the floor, were roughly cut pieces of semi-transparent glossy paper. They were pale blue and appeared to have formed part of an architect's plan. He hunted for bits with lettering on them and stuffed them into his pockets. Listening for the first sounds of Davina's return, he hastily rearranged the contents of the basket, and then turned his attention to the bureau. A large pair of scissors, like one at home strictly reserved for Jane's dressmaking, lay on the top of the heaps of letters and papers, but before he could examine these in any detail he heard a distant chink of china which sent him back to his chair. The next moment he rose politely once again as a trolley with coffee and cake was wheeled in.

He realised that to get the information he wanted it would be necessary to allow a cosy conversational atmosphere to develop, and endured being coyly fussed over as he was provided with refreshment. It was not difficult to introduce the subject of domestic problems in the seventies.

'Oh dear, no, I've no resident staff,' Davina told him. 'There haven't been any at the Manor for – let me think – six years, since an old retainer was pensioned off. But I'm lucky enough to have a real treasure of a daily. She's called Mrs Broom! Isn't it delightful? She comes for three hours every day, except at weekends. Of course she has to be fetched and taken home, but my brother and I manage between us.'

'You certainly are lucky, Miss Grant,' Pollard agreed, accepting a second cup of coffee. 'I suppose you have to do quite a lot of entertaining, don't you?'

She made a moue with her tight little mouth.

'Not nearly as much as I should, I'm afraid, for anyone in my position, but I'm trying to step it up. Between ourselves, my brother isn't much help to me. He really isn't interested in anything but sport, and at the moment he's simply absorbed in his engagement. Unfortunately Kate Ling hasn't had any experience of normal social life, as you'll have gathered for yourself, of course, so that doesn't help either.'

Pollard made a non-committal remark while deciding how best to extricate himself. He fell back on the time-honoured expedient of looking at his watch and exclaiming at the lateness of the hour.

'I must be starting off again,' he said. 'Inspector Toye will be wondering where I've got to.'

To his dismay Davina announced that she would walk up to the gates with him. As they set off, accompanied by Rex, he began to comment on the garden, and was astonished at the vehemence of her response.

'It's my worst headache,' she said. 'I *can't* find the time to work in it myself, and anyway I'm no good at gardening. And all the help I can get is a tiresome old man for two days a week. But it's got to be tidied up before the Fête. I'm *not* going to have people saying the place is going to pieces. I've had to get hold of a firm that sends round teams of gardeners, and it's going to cost the earth.'

Judging it expedient not to enquire about Heloise Grant's gardening activities, Pollard held forth at some length on the difficulties of getting gardening help in Wimbledon, managing to make the topic last until they arrived at the gates. To his alarm Davina seized his hand.

'It's been wonderful to meet again,' she told him with intensity.

Pollard contrived both to shake her hand briskly and detach his own.

'And many thanks for your hospitality, Miss Grant,' he replied cheerfully, 'and for giving me a chance to see inside your lovely house. Goodbye.'

He strode off down the hill with a sense of relief, and did not look back. So immature and gauche, poor girl, he thought, and pathetic, too. Sex-starved and status-starved ... But as he began to assess the results of his visit, she dropped out of his mind.

One thing seemed clear. There had been no resident servants in April 1975. Assuming there were no visitors, the household had consisted only of Heloise Grant, Peter and Davina. This could only suggest that Davina was a likely writer of the anonymous letter about the cleaning of Peter's car during the night of 1 April. There was obviously tension between the brother and sister, but all the same, what could her motive have been? And there was also the point that much of the tension might be recent, arising from the engagement.

Pollard was suddenly struck by an idea. Suppose Davina had been hacking up plans for the subdivision of Upway Manor into two houses or flats, perhaps drawn up by Peter himself? It would be a sensible way of sharing their inheritance, providing each of them with a home. But it was easy to see that Davina would see in it a loss of her personal status. All the same, it really did seem far-fetched to suggest that she might be trying – very clumsily – to remove him from the scene by getting him involved in a homicide charge ...

Anxious to see if the fragments in his pockets actually were plans, Pollard walked purposefully back to Stoneham, his long legs covering the distance so rapidly that several people stared as he passed. At the police station he sat down and began to fit the pieces together. His instinct to snatch up the bits with lettering on them seemed to have paid off. He was still staring at part of the mutilated heading of the plan when Toye came in.

'If your wits aren't completely addled after an evening at the movies, come and look at this,' Pollard said. 'I fished it out of Miss Davina Grant's wastepaper basket while she was making me some coffee.'

'Ethulon,' Toye remarked, looking down at the table.

'Come again?'

'It's the paper stuff architects draw out their plans on.

84

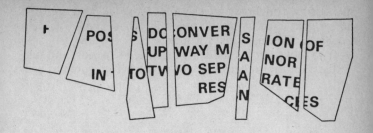

POSSIBLE CONVERSION OF UPWAY MANOR INTO TWO SEPARATE RESIDENCES

I've got a brother-in-law working in an architect's office.'

'Quite right. And I swear that it's a plan for converting Upway Manor into two units, to use the planners' jargon: one for Peter Grant and his bride-elect, and one for Davina. And obviously she isn't on. I listened outside the window to her chopping up the plan with a dirty great pair of scissors.'

'What would the legal position be, seeing the place was left to them both?' Toye asked.

'This is it. I suppose it would depend to some extent on the wording of the aunt's will. I don't know that it's really very important from our point of view, after all. From what I gathered tonight she and her brother aren't on the same wavelength, especially over his engagement to Kate Ling, but somehow I can't see her writing that letter. If he's mixed up in our chap's death it's bound to be darned unpleasant for her: not at all right for the Lady of Upway Manor image she's cultivating so hard. On the other hand it doesn't seem very likely that anyone besides the aunt and Peter and Davina Grant were in the house on 1 April '75.'

'That throws us back on somebody snooping from the gate, then?'

'Yes. We've only got to check up on everybody in the neighbourhood and all the Easter holiday crowd. We don't seem to be making much headway, do we? Still, Peter Grant'll turn up here at twelve tomorrow. I left him my card with a polite but very definite request. And I'll be surprised if that old bastard Geoffrey Ling doesn't make a move, so we ought soon to get that loose end tied up. If he hasn't contacted us by the time we've had breakfast, we'll get on to Akerman, just for luck.'

Toye looked at his suddenly dispirited superior, and suggested a return to their hotel for a beer before going to bed.

Chapter 7

When Pollard and Toye went round to the police station after breakfast on the following morning they found a good deal of activity in progress. Official and civilian cars were entering and leaving the car park, while inside the building purposeful footsteps echoed in the corridors. The door of Superintendent Crookshank's office was half open, and he was visible in deep discussion with the chief constable. Round a corner they ran into Inspector Hemsworthy.

'Fight at a back-street pub,' he told them. 'We get one every so often. Thugs from Wintlebury come over on their bikes spoiling for a punch-up. Two of our chaps were hurt this time, and one of 'em's still in hospital.'

Pollard commiserated, and went on with Toye to their room. No messages had come through, so he proceeded to ring George Akerman. A quiet, rather dry voice replied by repeating the telephone number.

'Mr Akerman? Superintendent Pollard here, in charge of the enquiry into the finding of the skeleton at Starbarrow. Could you spare me a few minutes this morning? I understand you've a very detailed knowledge of Cattesmoor, and it could help us to clear up one or two points. I can come along and see you, if that's convenient.'

'Quite convenient, Superintendent. I shall be working in my flat all the morning. It's in the house on the works site in Old Bridge Street.'

Pollard thanked him, and said that he expected to be along within the next hour.

'Misleading things, voices,' he remarked to Toye after ringing off. 'Akerman doesn't sound in the least like a chap who tramps all over the countryside, or a successful businessman either. Oh, good morning, sir,' he said, getting up as the chief constable's head came round the door. 'Sorry to hear you've got the aftermath of a Saturday night pub brawl on your hands.'

'Rather a nasty business as a matter of fact,' Henry Landfear replied as he sat down heavily. 'We've got the ringleaders, though, and there's a special sitting of the Bench at eleven. Would to God I were Home Secretary . . . However, you've troubles of your own. How's it going?'

Pollard summarised the developments of the past few days.

'It's an unsatisfactory sort of case,' he concluded. 'I feel all the time that there are undercurrents which I haven't managed to identify so far. We're having a go at Peter Grant later this morning. I'm hoping Kate Ling will have done a bit of spadework there.'

Henry Landfear grunted.

'For what it's worth I can't see young Grant being mixed up in this business. Not in character. Of course one can be devastatingly wrong about people.'

'What do you make of his sister, sir?' Pollard asked.

'I've hardly come across her. My wife thinks she ought to have gone off to a job and struck out on her own. Bit overshadowed by her aunt at home. Not that Heloise Grant would have meant it. She was damn good to both of 'em. Their father died about ten years ago. And they've come in for a packet now she's gone. No, even if the girl's digging in as mistress of the house and whatever, writing anonymous letters to put us on to her brother seems a bit improbable.'

'This is all very helpful, sir. Can you give us a line on Mr Akerman?'

'Akerman?' George Landfear paused to assemble his ideas. 'He's one of these conservationists: National Trust, Preservation of Rural England – the lot. Quite a big noise on the area committees. Locally he runs the Friends of Cattesmoor, especially now that Heloise Grant's gone. All this is in his spare time. He owns and runs a thriving printing works in the town, called Letterpress. It used to be a one-horse show which he bought when he moved down here about 1960, I think. It's a mystery how he gets so much done. Partly because he's a solitary sort of bloke, I suppose.'

'Is he married?' Pollard asked.

'Rumour has it that his wife walked out on him and he divorced her. He lives on his own down at the works. Well, I suppose I'd better be getting back to our squalid thugs. Glad to have had a word with you. You seem to have some useful irons in the fire. Let us know if you want any odd jobs done, of course.'

Henry Landfear lumbered to his feet and departed. After consulting a plan of Stoneham, Pollard and Toye went out to their car and set off for the Letterpress works. They found them in an area of small factories engaged in light industry on the north side of the town. The gates on to the site had apparently been unlocked for them, and they drove in past a small modern factory building to an adjoining and very ugly house of dingy red brick. The ground floor of this seemed to be occupied by offices, but a side door had a card inscribed 'G. R. Akerman' over a bell push. Pollard rang, and almost at once there was a sound of footsteps coming downstairs. The door was opened by a tall man in a pale blue drip-dry shirt.

'Superintendent Pollard?' he queried. 'I'm Akerman. Come along up.'

Pollard introduced Toye, and they followed up a short flight of stairs to a first-floor flat, and into a large living room which occupied the full width of the house. Its main windows faced west with a superb view across to Cattesmoor.

'You know, there's a lot to be said for living right on the job,' George Akerman remarked, as if reading Pollard's thoughts. 'It's timesaving, and quiet as the grave here at nights when the lads have knocked off. Not a fashionable neighbourhood admittedly, but at any rate there's room to move in these old-fashioned houses.'

Pollard agreed. George Akerman's life style clearly demanded plenty of space. At the far end of the room was a large filing cabinet, and an enormous working table at the moment covered with Ordnance Survey maps. Bookcases lined the walls and books were stacked on sundry

88

small tables. The room also had wall-to-wall carpeting, central heating, exceedingly comfortable armchairs and a colour TV set.

A reference to Isabel Dennis established a friendly atmosphere, and the conversation moved on easily to the Possel Way. As George Akerman talked, Pollard observed him closely. It was a narrow face with a determined chin, and hazel eyes which gave the impression of careful concentration on the matter in hand. It lit up attractively with an occasional smile, but in general its expression was guarded, Pollard thought, and he wondered briefly about the wife alleged to have walked out.

'Well, Mr Akerman,' he said pleasantly, taking advantage of a pause, 'we know you're a very busy man and mustn't take up your time. It's quite a small matter. We've been told of all your work for the preservation of Cattesmoor, and especially of its prehistoric monuments which you inspect regularly. Were you by any chance up on the moor doing just this on the Monday or Tuesday after Easter last year?'

'I can say right away that I was on the Monday,' George Akerman replied. 'I make a point of it on bank holidays. Unfortunately, some of the youngsters who come down to these parts on holiday are bloody little vandals, smashing things up just for the hell of it. We've had trouble, so I feel it's worth being around, although one can't be everywhere at once, of course. I'm not sure about the Tuesday off hand: I'll just look up last year's diary.'

'Do you close the works for both days?' Pollard asked.

'Yes. The chaps like the good long weekend, and we knock a day off the summer closure in lieu.' George Akerman extracted a bound desk diary from a shelf and stood flicking over the pages. 'No, I didn't go up on the Tuesday. I worked at home, partly down in the office, and partly up here.' He replaced the diary and returned to his chair.

'Of course you'll have followed the Press reports of the enquiry,' Pollard went on, 'and will realise that we're doing our utmost to trace the youth seen at the old lookout, at about a quarter to one on that Easter Monday. He was making for Biddle Bay along the cliffs, and when next seen

– except by a person or persons at present unknown – had been reduced to a skeleton and deposited in the kistvaen at Starbarrow.'

'You're absolutely satisfied on the identity question?' George Akerman asked.

'Absolutely. And although the pathologist's further report won't be officially out until later today, we're also absolutely satisfied about where the poor blighter spent the interval between death and premature resurrection: in a disused well at Starbarrow Farm.'

'Good God! The old well?' George Akerman, who had been following with the closest attention, stared at Pollard. 'Hence the miscellaneous deposits on the bones, of course.'

'You know about this well?'

'Yes. I knew Danby Blake a bit – the chap Ling bought the farm from – and he asked me out to lunch once. He told me he'd tried to get a better water supply by deepening an old well, but that it would have had to go deeper than he could afford to bore, and he'd had to scrap the idea and fill in the shaft.'

'Can we go back to that Easter Monday again?' Pollard asked. 'Did your tour of inspection take you anywhere near where our chap would have got to? And if it did, have you the slightest recollection of seeing a smallish long-haired type humping his gear on his back?'

'I'd have noticed him all right if he'd been within sighting distance,' George Akerman replied. 'He sounds just the sort one tries to keep an eye on. But if he didn't leave the lookout until a quarter to one, he couldn't possibly have got to the Biddle area where I was by early afternoon. Come and look at a map.'

They all migrated to the far end of the room, and George Akerman showed them his route up on to the western end of Cattesmoor. He had driven to Biddle Bay and gone on through the town, along the cliff road and past the outlying farms to where the surfaced road ended. He had then parked his car, and continued on foot to inspect a stone circle.

'This one,' he said, indicating it with a pencil.

'The Wanton Wenches,' Pollard read aloud. 'Sounds all right.'

90

'One of our best local names, I always think. It's interesting historically, too. Puritanism interpreting a Bronze Age monument about two and a half millennia later. The usual bit of folklore about girls dancing on a Sunday and being literally petrified by an irate Almighty. It's a lovely circle, although two of the stones have had to be re-erected. Well, I ate my sandwiches, and went on another half-mile to look at a standing stone, and then, as nobody was about, I decided to push off. At that point I was about twenty miles from the lookout.'

'Did you call it a day and go home?'

There was a slight pause. George Akerman let the pencil he was holding drop on the table.

'No,' he said. 'I drove back as far as Churstow, and then up on to the moor again, and along to Starbarrow. Then I—'

He broke off at the bleeping of a telephone and strode down the room to answer it. Pollard gave Toye a quick look, and appeared absorbed in map study while listening intently. He learnt nothing of the caller's identity however. George Akerman merely gave his number, and after a couple of seconds said without a trace of interest or pleasure in his voice that he had callers and would ring back shortly. As he returned to the table Pollard looked up at him.

'About what time was it when you got to the farm?' he asked.

'Roughly about three, I think. I was up there for half an hour or so.' George Akerman rested a foot on a rung of his chair and contemplated Pollard. 'I expect you're wondering why I went there. Partly to vet the kistvaen, but the main object of the exercise was to spy out the land for the late Miss Grant. She was President of the Friends of Cattesmoor, and as secretary I worked closely with her. She had been keen on reopening the Possel Way for walkers for years, but the difficulty was that parts of its route were only vaguely known. Then, a few years ago, a fellow doing historical research found a document which established that it ran behind Starbarrow Farm, and that there was a chapel there used by the pilgrims.' George Akerman paused to smile reminiscently. 'Well, Miss Grant simply took the bit between her teeth. She had left the Friends £5,000 in her will, and privately decided to make them an immediate donation of the money instead, to spend on re-establishing Possel if it was practicable. Unfortunately, in the meantime Geoffrey Ling had bought the farm, and it was soon perfectly obvious that we'd have to take him to court to get a right of way through his land. Naturally neither Miss Grant nor I were anxious to do this unless we'd got a really good case. She found out that the Lings were away over Easter, and asked me to go up and see exactly where the path would have to go, and what chance Ling would have of pleading invasion of his privacy and so on.'

'Did you by any chance notice the well?' Pollard asked.

'Yes. I came on it when I was looking round in the newtake.'

'This is important,' Pollard said. 'Try to visualise it, will you? Did the sheet iron covering it look as though it had recently been moved?'

George Akerman stared hard at the wall behind the table.

'No,' he said. 'Definitely not. I can see it quite clearly. Chunks of rock were piled on it, and the grass and stuff had grown over the edges.'

'Returning to our hiker who was going to end up there,' Pollard said. 'If you were only at Starbarrow between three and half-past, he obviously couldn't have made it. Did you by any chance see any other walkers about?'

'Nobody at all. I was rather relieved, to tell you the truth, as I was blatantly trespassing. I was surprised that I didn't meet anyone, but it was an early Easter, and there are never so many people around when that happens.'

Pollard looked at the map again.

'Have you got the sheet that shows the old tin workings?' he asked. 'It's been suggested that our chap may have spent the Monday night there.'

George Akerman hunted out another map from the assortment on the table.

'They're on this one. It seems a reasonable idea. Some of the buildings would give you quite a bit of shelter.'

'He could have hiked on to Starbarrow easily on the

Tuesday, I suppose?'

'Oh, yes. It would only be about half a dozen miles. But I should have thought it would have been more likely that he'd go back to the cliffs and try to make Biddle. Types like that usually hang around towns when they can.'

'The police over there are trying to pick up his trail,' Pollard said, 'but no luck so far. It's the heck of a long time ago for people to remember a stray youth ... Well, Mr Akerman, you've cleared up some points for us, anyway, and we're grateful. We'll press on and leave you in peace.'

A few minutes later they drove out of the gates into an empty street flanked on both sides by blank-eyed factories.

'Anything strike you?' Pollard asked Toye.

'It's as deserted here as out on the moor on a Sunday morning.'

'And quiet as the grave after working hours, Akerman said, didn't he? Not to mention bank holidays, of course. Miss Grant's dead, and there's not a soul to contradict his story about how he spent those two days. Not that there's the least suggestion that he was involved with the hippy ... Oh, hell, if only we could get a breakthrough of some sort, and find out what this bloody case is all about.'

'There's young Grant coming along in half an hour,' Toye suggested hopefully.

'Somebody else who'll freely admit having been up at Starbarrow at the critical time, and with a perfectly good innocent reason,' Pollard retorted gloomily, and relapsed into silence.

Canteen coffee did nothing to boost his morale, and it was only with an effort that he roused himself to find a fresh slant on the enquiry while waiting for Peter Grant to arrive. Slowly he began to work backwards along the line of the people they had interviewed, as though they were standing before him on parade. George Akerman, geographically isolated and socially detached in the midst of his many activities. Davina Grant, ambitious for status, determined, almost comically immature and quite oblivious of the fact, poor girl. Probably developing a crush on Akerman. Kate Ling. A grand girl there, and the most improbable product of her brilliant clown of a father and oddly detached mother. Ted Callington of the Mayfield Garage, whose personality and sales patter Toye had conveyed so well. Danby Blake, philosophical and undaunted. The Hawkins troupe, voluble but quite unshakeable and Mum-dominated. The local chaps: Henry Landfear, Crookshank . . .

At this point he halted. Pollard, suddenly alerted, concentrated on the saturnine countenance of the dour but basically likeable superintendent. He waited, but memory remained obstinately silent, and moved on again. Aunt Is, bless her. Right back to the beginning now, and the group standing ill at ease round the kistvaen. Davina Grant again, throwing her weight about, and the grey-headed Bill Worth with his barbed comments . . .

'Mr Peter Grant to see you, Mr Pollard, sir,' a constable announced from the door.

'Damn!' Pollard exclaimed, so vehement at the interruption that Toye looked at him in astonishment. 'Show him in, will you?'

The physical resemblance between Peter and Davina Grant was striking at first sight. They had the same rounded and rather full type of face, hazel eyes and dark hair. But there was nothing pursed or secretive about his mouth, and nothing of her latent tension in his open expression, although at the moment he looked worried.

'I suppose I've been a complete fool not to come and see you off my own bat, Superintendent,' he said. 'My girl says so, anyway. She's Kate Ling, as you know. Perhaps you'd take a look at these.'

Pollard mentally awarded Kate Ling an accolade, and read the two letters. They were all in the now familiar block capitals and on the same unidentifiable stationery. The envelopes were marked PERSONAL. One informed Peter Grant that his visit to Starbarrow Farm on 31 March 1975 was known to the writer, and that it was obvious why he had got rid of his car so quickly. The other was abusive and asked when he had hidden the body.

'When and where did you get these?' Pollard asked.

'The one about going out to the farm and the car came to the office by the second post on Friday, and the other one on Saturday. We don't open on Saturdays, but after

94

getting the first one I was a bit het up, and went along to see if another had come.'

'Are these letters the only reason why you haven't been along to see us, Mr Grant?'

'Well, no.' The young man shifted his position and looked embarrassed.

'Suppose we help you out a bit. I suggest that when you first heard that a skeleton had been found in the Starbarrow kistvaen, it may have crossed your mind that it could have been a practical joke carried out by your prospective father-in-law.'

'Well, it did actually. Then when there were those broadcast appeals for information about the chap those people saw at the old lookout, I got a bit rattled. I mean I didn't think for a moment that – that Mr Ling had bumped anyone off, but it did look as though the skeleton had come from the farm. It would have been damned difficult to get it to the kistvaen from anywhere else without being seen, let's face it. Then the next day – Friday – I got that letter myself, and it was a pretty nasty jolt. You see, it was true.'

'What was true?' Pollard enquired.

'I *had* been out to the farm on that Easter Monday when the hiker bloke whose skeleton it is, according to the papers, was last seen, and I was there pretty late, too.'

'How late, Mr Grant?'

'About six. I'd been playing in an Easter Monday tennis tournament at Biddle Sports Club and went up on the way back, just to see that the house was O.K. I'd promised Kate and her mother.'

'About six,' Pollard said thoughtfully. 'Did you see anyone around up on the moor?'

'Not a soul. It was beginning to get dark. I just tried the doors and vetted the windows and came away.'

'About your car,' Pollard went on after a short pause. 'I see no harm in telling you that we have had an anonymous letter advising us to ask you why you were cleaning your old car in your garage up to midnight on the night of 1 April last year.'

Peter Grant stared at him appalled.

'My God!' he said hoarsely. 'That's true, too. Who on

earth *is* it who's got it in for me like this? I'd have said I hadn't an enemy in the world.'

'Why were you cleaning it so thoroughly?' Pollard pressed him.

'I was going to trade it in the next morning. I'd been wanting a new car for ages, and when I heard I was being taken on by our firm as a partner a couple of weeks before Easter, Aunt Heloise was so bucked that she said she'd foot the bill as soon as I saw something I really liked. It wasn't a particularly good time just over Easter, but on the Tuesday evening – 1 April, I mean – I went to fill up with petrol at the Mayfield, and George Fry, a foreman who's an old buddy of mine, came out and told me that a super B.M.W. had just been delivered from the works. We went to look at it, and I decided on the spot that I'd have it. So of course I put in the evening tarting up my Marina . . . I suppose you won't believe a word of this,' he concluded desperately.

'Why not, Mr Grant? It's a perfectly credible story, and can be checked by the foreman if necessary. Before you go, how did you spend Tuesday, 1 April? Did you go over to Starbarrow again by any chance?'

Peter Grant shook his head.

'We started up at the office again on the Tuesday. I remember it quite well because it was my first normal day as a partner, and it felt rather good. I coped with my mail, and then my secretary helped me shift into my new room, and I had an early snack and went off to a site meeting at a place called Candlebridge, where we're building a factory. It's about thirty miles east of Stoneham. The meeting went on until about four, and then I came back to the office to finish things up, and then knocked off and went to the Mayfield for petrol, as I told you.'

'Did you go out to Starbarrow again before the Lings came back on the following Friday?'

'No, I didn't. Naturally I can't remember at this distance of time what work I was doing, but there'd be a record at the office. I realise you'll have to approach the senior partners, but they're jolly decent chaps, so it's O.K. by me.'

Pollard glanced across at Toye.

'Got all that, Inspector? Well, Mr Grant, we'll have a

statement typed out for you to read over and sign if you consider it's a true record. Perhaps you'd look in tomorrow morning? You'll understand that we have to check up on what you've told us, but it'll be done discreetly. And one more thing. As you say, someone does seem to be out for your blood, so watch out within reason.'

Peter Grant drew the back of his hand across his forehead.

'You've been awfully decent,' he said. 'Thanks a lot. It all seems so unreal, somehow. I can hardly take it in.'

'I suppose you've no idea who this someone could possibly be?'

'Absolutely none. It simply doesn't mean a thing to me.'

'When are you and Miss Ling getting married?' Pollard asked more conversationally as they got up.

'There's a bit of a hold-up over the house,' Peter Grant said, frowning slightly. 'Our aunt left Upway to my sister and myself jointly, and the obvious thing is to divide it into two. I've done plans and got them through the district planning committee, and given them to my sister to study in detail, but she's not at all keen on the idea, and doesn't want me to buy her out. In fact, she's offered to buy me out, but that just isn't on. There've been Grants at Upway for two hundred years, and I hope a son of mine'll carry on some day. However, I expect we'll get things sorted out in time.'

When Toye returned from seeing Peter Grant off he found Pollard gently tilting his chair backwards and forwards with an inscrutable expression on his face.

'Reactions?' he queried, coming to a halt.

'I reckon we can count him out over the chap's death,' Toye said, sitting on the edge of the table. 'Maybe he's a good architect, but he hasn't got what it takes to lead the likes of us up the garden path. Mind you, we'll have to check on him,' he added with characteristic caution.

'Not much we can do about it on a Sunday afternoon,' Pollard replied. 'Still, it's nice to feel we've got a definite programme for tomorrow. Another thing is that it seems to me to explain Ling's caginess about the period when the farm was shut up. He's no fool at all, and I expect he soon tumbled to it that Grant had been going out there. The young couple may even have told him when they got engaged. Pulling his leg, so to speak. Then, after he'd dumped the skeleton in the kistvaen as a huge joke, out comes the report that it was only about a year old, and he suddenly realises the possible implications and gets cold feet . . . Look here, I've got the ghost of an idea at the back of my mind. A drink might get it to walk. Let's go along to that pub down the road and have a bar snack. The Red Lion, or something, isn't it?'

Half an hour later they were coming out of the pub when they met a party just arriving. It was headed by a buxom ginger-haired woman in a frock loudly patterned in emerald green and lemon yellow. She stared and beamed broadly.

'Why, it's the detective gentleman,' she exclaimed. 'Look Sam, the gentleman from Scotland Yard we saw up at the police station. Pleased to meet you again, sir.'

Shaking hands with Mr and Mrs Hawkins, the latter's sister and brother-in-law and young Tommy was inevitable. Pollard gathered that Linda and her boy friend were off on their own.

'Well, we never thought we'd be meetin' you again, sir, did we, Sam?' Mrs Hawkins rattled on. 'And we nearly went to the Queen's Head, too. You never know, do you? Why, that picnic we had up to the lookout when we saw the hippy. We all but went over to Biddle Bay that Easter Monday, and up to the lookout on the Tuesday, seeing that Sam had both days off. But Linda fancied the picnic at the lookout, and as she only had the one day, that settled it. We had a nice day at Biddle on the Tuesday, though, and saw Mr Akerman who's Sam's boss drivin' through in the afternoon, didn't we, Sam? Doin' one of his rounds up on Cattesmoor, I daresay. Very keen on what they calls conservation, he is.'

Mr Hawkins made an inarticulate assenting sound.

'Mr Akerman?' Pollard said, simulating merely polite interest. 'You'd expect him to be up there on a bank holiday when there are more vandals around.'

'Maybe he was there on the Monday, too. But he was drivin' back towards Stoneham that Tuesday afternoon, wherever he'd bin. Pointed him out to you and Bert, didn't I, Margie?'

'That's right,' her sister agreed.

'I saw 'n too,' Tommy Hawkins suddenly contributed in a bass growl. 'Drivin' 'is old Volvo Estate. Got a posh new one soon after we saw'n.'

Chapter 8

Even the habitually cautious Toye agreed that the unanimous evidence of the Hawkins family would stand up in court.

'It's the girl only having the Monday off that settles it,' he said. 'They just can't have made a mistake about the day they saw Akerman at Biddle Bay being the Tuesday.'

Pollard, who had been pacing restlessly in their room at the police station, came to a halt with his back to the window and his elbows resting on the sill.

'Let's assume for the moment that Akerman did kill our bloke somewhere beyond Biddle, and brought the body back by car and hid it in the well at Starbarrow Farm,' he said. 'He only just didn't get away with it, but it was madly risky. He's quite well-known in this part of the world, and people have days out and go places over the Easter holiday. Why did he lie about the day he did the job? Switching the Monday and the Tuesday round was a clever idea when we started asking awkward questions. After fifteen months people get a bit hazy about when they happened to see X pass in his car, unless there's some particular reason to fix it in their minds. It's now common knowledge that we're working on the assumption that the Starbarrow skeleton's that of the chap seen at the lookout soon after midday on Easter Monday. He was hiking, and couldn't have got to the Biddle area till about midday on Tuesday. All right. Akerman states that he was working at home all day on Tuesday, having done a round on Cattesmoor on Monday. Time's been on his side. The chances of anyone remembering seeing him coming or going in that industrial desert where he lives are pretty well nil.'

Toye looked up from the maps spread out on the table.

'Our chap could have got to somewhere near Biddle by Tuesday midday, but Akerman's timing seems a bit rum. He says he got to Biddle about eleven. It wouldn't have taken more than about a quarter of an hour to drive through it, and up the cliff road till it comes to an end, and on a bit further into the moor. Wouldn't our chap have kept along the cliffs? Surely that's where they'd have met? Bit public for murdering someone and stowing him into your bus, don't you think? A car full of picnickers could have followed on any minute. And if Akerman had luck and nobody turned up, why did he hang about so long? The Hawkins lot saw him driving back about half-past two, they said.'

Pollard detached himself from the window sill and came across to the table for another look at the maps.

'After the coast road peters out there's a rough track for a bit,' he said, 'but it's not a foregone conclusion that our bloke came along it. If he camped at the tin workings on the Monday night, the shortest way on to Biddle was to cut across country and strike the road on the outskirts. One side of a triangle instead of two. Brush up your Euclid, in fact. If he did that, he'd have passed very near the Wanton Wenches circle – might even have stopped off at it for a rest. Akerman was going there, and it would have been a much more secluded place for bumping anyone off. See?'

As he spoke, he laid a pencil on the map to illustrate his point. Toye agreed, with reservations.

'I'll grant you all that, sir,' he said, 'but if he did bump the chap off, how could he have got the body back to his car?'

'Akerman could have been lying about parking the car and walking a couple of miles out to the circle. He might have driven right up to it. Let's go and see if it's a physical possibility, shall we? . . . What's up? Oh, I see: the thought of crashing the car over boulders and sinking it up to the axle in bogs. Go and see if we can borrow the Land Rover again. Anyway, it's an excuse for getting out of here for the afternoon: it's like being in an oven.'

Toye vanished with alacrity. Pollard mopped his forehead, and wondered if the heat was affecting his brain. The Akerman development seemed to raise more problems rather than solve existing ones. Could it have been a pre-arranged meeting with the hippy, implying a previous link, so far undiscovered? If not, what could have led a man of Akerman's type to kill a stranger on sight? A violent punch-up seemed ruled out by the absence of any bone injury: the skeleton's skull had been most meticulously examined. A knife? Would Akerman have been carrying round a knife? Suppose the hippy had a heart attack? Well, then, why not contact an ambulance, and say you'd found the poor devil lying on the ground?

At the sound of activity in the car park Pollard got up abruptly and left these queries unanswered. After all, the case against George Akerman was based on pure supposition at the moment. He went out of the building into the blinding glare of the early afternoon, a wave of heat seeming to rise from the ground and hitting him. The Land Rover drew up with Toye at the wheel. With a pair of sunglasses clipped to his hornrims he looked even more like a meditative owl than usual.

They were soon out on the now familiar road to Biddle Bay. It was surprising what new significance it had taken on since that early morning run into Stoneham with Aunt Is less than a fortnight ago, Pollard thought. Churstow, which he had hardly registered, was now the approach to the sparking-off point of the whole business: Starbarrow Farm and the kistvaen. There, up the Holston turning, was the cottage where Aunt Is's remark about aerial photography had led to such an important breakthrough. Just short of Biddle Bay the road to Winnage and Danby Blake branched off. As they drove into the seaside resort he considered a call at the police station, but decided against it. Obviously local enquiries about the hippy set in motion by Superintendent Pratt had drawn a blank so far.

Toye negotiated the crowded sea front with some difficulty, and they bore right and began to climb steeply on the cliff road. They passed houses and bungalows at which the hippy might have called, and the two farms with deterrent notices about dogs on their gates. Farther on again, numerous cars were parked along railings, their passengers enjoying the view out to sea in the intervals of sleeping and reading the Sunday papers. Finally the tarmac surface of

101

the road ended. A few cars had driven farther along a stony track and their more enterprising inmates were sitting out among the heather where any patches of shade could be found.

'People seem to have struck off into the moor here,' Toye said. 'See those wheel marks?'

'O.K.,' Pollard replied. 'Head roughly in that direction: east-south-east. I'll guide you from the map.'

They advanced slowly, sometimes diverging from their course to avoid rocks and dense clumps of gorse. A herd of grazing cattle raised their heads as they passed and stared curiously at the Land Rover, but there was no other sign of life. After about a mile and a half Pollard called a halt.

'I'll just shin up that rock pile and see if I can spot the Wenches,' he said.

Massive horizontal slabs provided foot and hand holds, and he was soon standing on the flat top. A couple of hundred yards ahead, on a gentle slope leading to a col between two rocky hillocks, was a circle formed by nine upright stones varying between four and six feet in height. Whether by accident or design they all heeled over a little in a clockwise direction, giving the impression of a lively round dance in progress, and in some way this was enhanced by their shadows of varying length, all pointing north-eastwards. For a few moments Pollard stood fascinated. Then with an effort he switched his attention to the practical problem of how near the circle it would be possible to get the Land Rover.

'I'll go ahead on foot,' he told Toye on coming down. 'We can get quite a bit closer.'

He walked on slowly, picking out the best route for the car and studying the surface intently. Was it imagination, or were there signs that a vehicle or vehicles had come this way before: a slight flattening of the grass here, and a broken stem of bracken there? Not that it need have been Akerman's car, of course. There were plenty of people interested in archaeology around these days ... Anyway, did murderers revisit the scene of their crime? He had always been inclined to think that they did, endlessly tormented by the fear of having overlooked some vital clue to their identity.

The traces, real or imagined, led him to an outcrop of rock beyond which the ground sloped up gently to the col and the Wanton Wenches. The Land Rover lurched along in his wake and came to a halt. Toye got out, and they walked towards the circle of stones. In the wide context of empty moor and cloudless sky it had a quality of emphasis. Toye eyed it disapprovingly.

'Heathenish,' he commented.

'It's saying something that seemed important at the time,' Pollard replied. 'Pity the girls can't talk.' He stood in the centre of the circle and turned round slowly, looking at the stones one by one. 'What's happened to that bosomy one over there?' He walked across to the most massive of the nine, and saw that it was blacked by smoke down one side. Attempts had been made to clean it, but the scorch marks remained. Rubbing with a moistened finger had no effect.

'Look at this,' Toye said, who was examining the grass at the foot of the stone. 'Turves have been cut out and replaced.'

None of the remaining stones were damaged. They returned to the car to get some shade and discuss their findings.

'Summing it all up,' Pollard said, 'I'm pretty sure that a car or cars have been out here, and obviously some vandal lit a fire by that stone. Somebody has done his or her best to clear up the mess. This may have nothing whatever to do with our case. Keen amateur archaeologists may have read about the circle and come out to see it. Vandals do get around, unfortunately, and Akerman would naturally try to repair any damage done by them. On the other hand, Akerman lied about the day he came out here, and may have lied about what he did when he arrived. Suppose he drove out instead of walking the last couple of miles, and came on our chap cooking up a snack on a fire he'd lit by that stone. Akerman sees red, beats him up and kills him, probably not intending to. Gets him by the throat and shakes him to death, or something of that sort which wouldn't cause a bone injury. There's nobody within miles, so he lugs the body to his car, stows it inside with a rug over it, collects all the clobber and bungs it into the boot, stamps the fire out, considers his next step and gets an inspiration. He has to go up to Starbarrow Farm, so why not dump the corpse in the old well? All this will have taken time, so his story of having walked to the circle and gone on further to look at a standing stone will account for his not going through Biddle Bay until half-past two. How's that?'

Toye considered deeply.

'He admitted knowing about the well, didn't he?'

'Yes, he said Danby Blake had told him about it. Besides, the farm was empty for several years, and I'm sure the Friends of Cattesmoor did some poking about. My guess is that he'd had a good look at it.'

For a couple of minutes they sat in silence, thinking things over.

'There's one thing I'd've done, if I'd been Akerman and had killed the bloke,' Toye said suddenly.

'Don't tell me,' Pollard said, suddenly grinning. 'He'd have changed his car! Right. First thing tomorrow we'll get Crookshank on to the licensing people again. If he did, not long after Easter last year, I shall begin to think that we've got the makings of a case. There's another point that's just struck me. Does Akerman report damage of these ancient monuments to the Friends' Committee? I remember Aunt Is saying that vandals had pulled down a wayside cross. It would be interesting to know if and when he reported this fire at the Wanton Wenches. I'll ring her when we get back. Tempting to stop off at Holston for a cuppa, but least said, best, at the moment, I think.'

There being nothing further of any use to be done on the spot, they lumbered back to the cliff road and started for Stoneham. On arriving at the police station they were greeted with the news that Mr Ling of Starbarrow Farm, Churstow, was waiting to see Superintendent Pollard. Asked how he had got on with the gentleman, the duty sergeant cast up his eyes to the ceiling and shrugged. Mr Ling had been a bit put out at having to wait.

'He can damn well wait a bit longer,' Pollard said. 'A cuppa – several cuppas – are a must. We've been sweating it out on Cattesmoor ... I suppose Grant went out to the farm from here, and told them he'd been questioned. Kate

Ling has the wits to see that it's in his interest to clear up the whole business, and put pressure on her old man. She was certain that he'd put the skeleton in the kistvaen.'

A quarter of an hour later he drained a third large cup and looked at Toye.

'Over to you, old cock. Bring him in.'

Toye tidily collected the tea tray and disappeared. A few minutes later the door opened again.

'Mr Ling to see you, sir,' he announced impassively.

'Good evening, Mr Ling,' Pollard opened. 'I'm sorry you've had to wait. Please sit down.'

Geoffrey Ling planted himself on a chair and stared at him truculently, his lower lip characteristically out-thrust.

'I've come for the purpose of making a statement,' he announced. 'Take it down, will you? . . . I, Geoffrey Bruce Ling, of Starbarrow Farm, Churstow, in the county of—'

'Just a minute,' Pollard interrupted. 'There's an official formula: I, Geoffrey Bruce Ling wish to make a statement. I want someone to write down what I say. I have been told that I need not say anything unless I wish to do so, and that whatever I say may be given in evidence.'

'Is that all?' Geoffrey Ling enquired sarcastically. 'Balderdash, and jobs for the boys. Put the whole bloody preamble down if you like,' he added, turning to Toye . . . 'What, sign it? My God! . . . Now then, let's get on with it . . . I, Geoffrey Bruce Ling of Starbarrow Farm, Churstow, in the county of Glintshire, found a human skeleton in a disused well on my property on Saturday, 12 June last. I took it out, and during the night I put it in the Starbarrow kistvaen . . . Type it out, man, and I'll sign it.'

'Concise and to the point,' Pollard commented. 'What a nasty jolt you must have had when the post-mortem report came out, stating that death had occurred only a year or so ago. You already knew that Mr Peter Grant had visited the farm when you were all on holiday in late March and early April last year, didn't you? How did you discover this, by the way?'

'It came out in the besotted atmosphere of my daughter's engagement to him,' Geoffrey Ling replied complacently.

Recognising a doting father, Pollard waited.

'My daughter Kate,' Geoffrey Ling resumed, resting his hands on the table and leaning back in his chair, 'has elected to marry a blameless young man of little more than average ability. He plays the game, carries a straight bat, keeps a stiff upper lip and can be relied upon to do the decent thing. So be it. If you think him capable of committing a murder and concealing the corpse in a well belonging to his affianced's father, you're a bigger fool than I take you for, Mr Superintendent Pollard of New Scotland Yard.'

'In a case of homicide,' Pollard replied, 'it's obviously necessary to question anyone who could be responsible on grounds of physical possibility. This doesn't imply equating opportunity with guilt, but alibis have to be checked and statements verified. This is the present position in Mr Grant's case.'

Geoffrey Ling thumped the table angrily.

'Why pick on him? What about the bloody Friends of Cattesmoor, as they call themselves? How many of them came nosing round when it got about that we were away? That preposterous medieval document – probably a fake – had been found which lost me the right-of-way case in the end. I'd had a letter from Akerman, their secretary, suggesting that we meet to discuss the demarcation of the Possel Way through my newtake, and public access to the remains of the chapel. Naturally I wrote back telling him to go to hell. I'd stake everything I've got that he came along. Brought that damned woman Grant with him, I daresay. She was behind it all.'

There was a momentary silence before Pollard abruptly switched to another topic.

'What made you open up the old well, Mr Ling?'

'Because I saw somebody else had been monkeying about with the sheet iron cover. The last time I'd looked at it was when I bought the farm. It was partly covered with grass and weeds then.'

'The lie indirect,' Pollard said thoughtfully. 'When I asked you if you had arranged for anyone to come out to the farm while you were abroad, you said no, although you had since found out that your daughter had fixed with Mr Grant to keep an eye on the place. Asked about traces of unauthorised entry to your property, you denied having found any. Your defence there would be that you didn't know for certain that the well cover had been moved during that period.'

Geoffrey Ling grinned maliciously.

'Right on both counts. You can't get me on either of 'em. Well, get moving. I've made a statement. What are you going to charge me on?'

'Charge you?' Pollard's tone conveyed a lack of urgency. 'With failing to report finding human remains on your property? I rather doubt if that would be considered necessary. Or with deliberately obstructing the police in their enquiries? It's possible you might have to face a charge of that at some stage. But at the moment it's a matter of academic interest until we're satisfied that your statement stands up.'

Geoffrey Ling's expression of incredulity changed to one of furious indignation.

'What the hell do you mean?' he shouted. 'Haven't I made a formal statement and signed the blasted thing?'

'You have. It will be confirmed or disproved by the pathologist who is examining the bones and other things we found in the well, to see if they tie up with the skeleton. You wouldn't expect us to swallow your statement whole, surely, Mr Ling? You've quite a reputation for practical jokes, haven't you? Thank you for coming in. We needn't keep you any longer this evening. Inspector Toye, see Mr Ling out, will you?'

Toye returned shortly looking gratified.

'He went out faster than he came in,' he reported with satisfaction. 'Spot on, you were, sir. Disgraceful, the way he's obstructed us. It doesn't seem right to me for him to get away with it.'

'We've got bigger fish to fry, old chap,' Pollard said absently, without looking up from an elaborate doodle he was executing on the back of an envelope. 'Sorry, no joke intended.'

'Meaning Akerman, sir?'

'Akerman, anyway. If it turns out that he did change his car soon after Easter last year, I suppose we pull him in for questioning. But I'd feel a lot happier if something in the way of a motive emerged. At the moment there are so many unanswered questions, aren't there? If it was deliberate murder, how was it done and why? If there was some sort of accident, why on earth didn't a man of Akerman's status call the police? ... Why this fixed stare and furrowed brow?'

'You said "Akerman, anyway",' Toye insisted. 'Do you mean you think somebody else could be involved?'

Pollard hesitated.

'Yes, I think it's possible,' he said at last. 'As it stands at the moment his behaviour seems so motiveless. Only don't ask me who or how, will you? I haven't a clue. Well, anyhow, we'll start off tomorrow by checking Peter Grant's alibi. I'll leave a chit here for Crookshank, asking him to find out about any change of car by Akerman soon after Easter '75 ... Come in! Oh, here's the pathologist's report on the metatarsals and whatever ... Yes, they belong to the skeleton all right. I'm glad the report's only just come. I enjoyed deflating that old blighter Ling.'

He pulled the telephone towards him, grinning at the thought of how Isabel Dennis would have enjoyed the final stages of the Ling interview, and dialled her number.

'Tom again, Aunt,' he said. 'Can you supply a spot of gen? We're interested in any damage to the ancient monuments on Cattesmoor in the weeks after Easter last year. You said something about a wayside cross being pulled down, didn't you? Would there be reports of anything of this sort in the minutes of the Friends' Committee that might give an idea of when it happened?'

'Yes, there would,' Isabel Dennis replied. 'George Akerman always reports damage, and any making good he's had done. He may not have discovered it himself, but people let him know as the secretary if they find anything wrong. Hold on, and I'll have a look at last year's minutes: we meet on the third Wednesday of the month. The wayside cross business was the year before, though.'

Pollard covered the mouthpiece of the receiver with his hand as he waited.

'If you'd been Akerman, and we're right about what happened at the Wanton Wenches, how soon would you have reported the damage?' he asked Toye, who had been

108

listening in with interest.

'Not at the April meeting. Not unless someone else had written in about it. I wouldn't want to draw attention to the place so soon, just in case anybody'd seen anything of the hippy. I'd wait till the May meeting. That would be getting on for a couple of months after the Easter bank holiday when I'd normally have a look round, so it would be quite usual for me to be up on the moor again.'

'That's what I thought,' Pollard agreed. 'And after the Easter holiday there wouldn't be so many – hullo, yes, I'm still here, Aunt . . .'

No damage had been mentioned at the April 1975 committee, Isabel Dennis told him, but on 21 May George Akerman had reported that someone had lit a fire right up against one of the stones of the Wanton Wenches Circle at the Biddle Bay end of the moor. The stone was badly scorched, and the turf at the base burnt. This had been cut out and replaced, but little could be done about the stone . . .

Pollard commiserated, thanked her, and diverted the conversation into other channels. Finally he rang off, wondering if it had struck his astute aunt as surprising that he had not applied to George Akerman in his official capacity for the information.

Chapter 9

Roger Steadman, senior partner of Steadman, Hillard and Grant, Architects, had a beaky face, alert brown eyes and greying hair worn long enough to curl up at the back. The general effect was streamlined, and gave the impression that he had been stopped while in rapid movement. He sat looking incredulously at Pollard across his desk.

'Let me get this clear,' he said. 'Some type's been writing anonymous letters implying that Peter Grant' – he gave the name slight emphasis – 'is involved in the death of the chap whose skeleton turned up in the Starbarrow kistvaen. Right?'

'Dead right, Mr Steadman,' Pollard replied. 'We're now satisfied that the chap was seen at the old lookout on the cliffs on Easter Monday last year, and we're interested in the following Tuesday, Wednesday and Thursday. Mr Ling and his family returned home from a holiday abroad on the Friday, and the chances that the body was put into the disused well on the property after their return are remote. We're checking on anyone known to have been at Starbarrow Farm during that Easter week. Mr Peter Grant had an understanding with Miss Kate Ling that he would keep an eye on the house while it was empty, and admits that he was there on the evening of Easter Monday, on his way back from playing in a tennis tournament at Biddle Bay, but states that he did not visit the farm again before the Lings came back. He's given us an account of his movements on the Tuesday – 1 April, that is – but says he cannot remember what work he was doing on the two following days. Have you a record of his professional engagements?'

By this time Roger Steadman's incredulity had changed to indignation.

'This is absolutely preposterous!' he exclaimed. 'Not only the suggestion that he's implicated in a murder, but that anybody's making it. There's obviously some nut around. Still, I suppose it's your job to investigate this sort of thing. Yes, we keep our appointment books for a year or two. I'll ask for all of 'em to make it less obvious.'

He picked up a desk telephone and gave an order. In the rather uncomfortable silence which descended Pollard glanced round the room. Photographs and maps were pinned on the walls, and plans in preparation were spread out on a table in a window, amid a clutter of drawing implements and rolls of unused pale blue enkalon. The door opened to admit a secretary carrying three slim foolscap-size books in hard covers.

'Thanks, Miss Kellow,' Roger Steadman said, taking them. 'Keep everybody at bay for half an hour, will you?'

Before the door had closed behind her, he had opened one of the three desk diaries and was leafing through its pages.

'Week beginning Monday, 31 March, 1975,' he said

shortly. 'May I ask how long you assume it would take to drive out to Starbarrow Farm, kill somebody, get a cover off a disused well, chuck the body down the shaft, make everything good, and then get back?'

'At least three hours,' Pollard replied. 'Longer, if there was a row first.'

'Well then, you're going to find it bloody difficult to pin this murder on to Peter Grant, let me tell you. On Tuesday, 1 April, he started in as a partner in this firm. Previously he'd only been an assistant. I can swear that he spent the best part of the morning shifting to his new room with all his gear. In the afternoon he was due at a site meeting at Candleford at 2.30. That's thirty miles away, and he couldn't have been back here before 4.30, and would have his letters to sign, and so on. Bit late to start out at five unless he was going to finish the job in the dark, of course ... On the Wednesday morning we had a pretty lengthy partnership meeting, and went out to look at a site on the outskirts of the town. Grant had a client's appointment at 3.30, and was due at a Stoneham tennis club committee at 5.30. He's the secretary, incidentally. Naturally I can't swear that he went to the meeting, but you could ask the treasurer, James Cantripp. He's retired and lives at Churstow. On Thursday morning Grant had an appointment to meet a client at the chap's house, here in Stoneham, and a date with one of the Planning Committee at the Council Offices at 3.15. He came to supper at my house. My son, who's a friend of his, was home for the night. Take a look for yourself.'

Roger Steadman pushed the appointments book across the desk. Pollard studied it carefully.

'These ticks beside the professional engagements mean that they were kept, I take it?' he asked.

'Yes. One's secretary keeps a record. If you turn on a few pages you'll probably come to a fixture with a cross beside it, showing a cancellation.'

'Thanks,' Pollard said, returning the book. 'This confirms Mr Grant's statement, and seems conclusive, apart from the one point of the tennis club committee. I'm grateful for your co-operation, Mr Steadman.'

'Sorry if I've been a bit abrasive.' Roger Steadman held

out his cigarette case. 'But honestly, if you knew Peter Grant as I do . . . What a fantastic business it is. Macabre and mad, and the only handy *non-compos* type, old Ling, apparently not in the running at all. However, I mustn't talk out of turn. Obviously you can't discuss the situation. I suppose there's no other useful gen I could produce for you?'

'There's just one possibility that's occurred to me,' Pollard replied, 'and it's probably absurdly far-fetched. I suppose you can't think of a dissatisfied client who's a bit unbalanced, and has a grievance against Mr Grant? I'm thinking of the anonymous letters.'

'It's by no means all that far-fetched. You wouldn't believe how bloodyminded some clients can be if anything goes wrong, or even if it doesn't. But Peter's still quite a youngster, and one keeps in touch with him over his jobs, and I can't think of anyone at all who's got it in for him on professional grounds. And in his social life he's very popular locally. In fact, the only person I know of that he's having difficulty with is his sister, over at Upway Manor. Their aunt left it to them jointly – always a mistake, and likely to lead to trouble, in my opinion. Anyway, Peter wants to live there when he marries Kate Ling in August, and he's offered either to buy her out at a proper valuation, or have the place divided into two quite separate units. It lends itself perfectly well to sub-division, as it happens, and he's drawn up an excellent plan, but she seems to be digging her toes in.'

'Why?' Pollard probed. 'Surely it's far too large for her on her own?'

'She fancies herself as the sort of local leading lady that her aunt was. Competent benevolent finger in every pie – you know. It's ludicrous, of course. Old Heloise was a great girl, if a shade bossy, and Davina just hasn't got what it takes. I've advised Peter to stand his ground and consult his solicitors. However, I can't see Davina trying to get her brother charged with murder. She's a snob – the dated sort – and murder's still rather non-U, isn't it? By the way, does he know that you've been seeing me about his alibis?'

'You weren't mentioned personally, but he saw at once that I'd want access to office records.'

'Good. I'll try to buck him up. I hope you'll be able to give him an all-clear shortly?'

Pollard assured him that this would be done at the earliest possible moment, and left soon afterwards. He had hardly crossed the threshold when Peter Grant dropped out of his mind. He threaded his way through the shoppers crowding the pavements, oblivious of the occasional curious glances he attracted, his thoughts on his visit to Upway Manor. The scent of roses came back to him, and the feel of turf under his feet as he stood on the edge of the lawn, listening to the sharp irregular cutting sound coming from the lighted window open at the bottom. In response to an inner uneasiness he concentrated on the memory, but although so vivid it was non-productive. He found himself walking into the police station, and forcibly switched his attention to the outcome of Toye's visit to the Mayfield Garage.

Toye had already returned, and reported that Peter Grant had been in and signed his statement. He himself hadn't done too badly at the Mayfield Garage. George Fry, the foreman, remembered Mr Grant coming in just before knocking-off time on 1 April, last year, because of giving him a preview of the B.M.W. He'd fallen flat for it, and said he was going right back to put it to his auntie, old Miss Grant, and that he'd spend the evening tarting up his Marina before getting Mr Callington to have a look at it next day. Fry had repeated several times that Mr Grant was a real nice young chap, one of the best.

'I managed to bring the conversation round to changing your car,' Toye went on, 'and Fry had plenty to say about choosing your time, bearing in mind the make and the question of wear and tear. No sense in getting a brand new model every year if it was going to get the hell of a bashing the way you ran it. It'd pay you better to run your old one a bit longer if you weren't having trouble with it, as he'd told Mr Akerman. Of course, I didn't know a thing about Akerman, and got a long story about him driving all over Cattesmoor on this conservation racket, and insisting on trading in a roadworthy Volvo Estate last summer for a new one, against his – George Fry's – advice. I didn't press for exact dates.'

'Nice work,' Pollard said. 'We ought to get the exact date sometime this morning from the licensing people. I haven't done too badly either.'

He gave Toye the gist of his conversation with Roger Steadman, and they agreed that the job had better be rounded off by a visit to James Cantripp, treasurer of the Stoneham Tennis Club. It was settled that Toye should go out to Churstow, while Pollard made a provisional plan for tackling George Akerman.

As soon as he was alone Pollard flung himself down at the table, resting his elbows on it and cupping his chin in his hands. Why, he asked himself, had Davina Grant suddenly loomed up in his mind, ousting George Akerman from the centre of the stage? To his surprise and discomfiture his mind promptly came up with an answer: her pretensions and posturings had made her so ludicrous that he had not really taken her very seriously. Clumsy self-assertion, girlish infatuation for George Akerman, and hopeless lack of chic in spite of expensive clothes had added up to the stage figure of the frustrated spinster, always good for a laugh but little else. Mercifully his professional experience had now come to his rescue at last.

He turned over in his mind what Bill Worth, Henry Landfear and Roger Steadman had said about her. They had all drawn basically the same picture: a young woman outshone by a likeable, able and wealthy aunt. Limited and immature, tco, Pollard thought, but fanatically determined to make the grade. How did George Akerman fit in, he wondered? Davina Grant was obviously sexually and emotionally frustrated, and equally obviously throwing herself at his head. And Upway Manor was the essential setting for the life she was struggling to achieve ... hence her flat refusal either to share it with her brother or to let him buy her out ...

Pollard shifted his position and sat scowling at the opposite wall. All this added up, he decided, and fitted in with the anonymous letters and the telephone call about Peter washing his car. It had been a mistake to assume she had not been responsible for them because she would hardly want to involve him in a charge of homicide. Wasn't the game to get him talked about and discredited, so that he might decide to leave the neighbourhood, and agree to her buying his share of the house? Crude and clumsy, but so was she. Ruthless, too, Pollard thought, remembering the vicious destruction of the house conversion plans. Not for the first time he wondered about the respective contributions of heredity and environment to warped personalities. Perhaps Davina Grant's childhood had been difficult, and on top of it had come the shock of losing her parents even before the frustration of life with her aunt had started. The phrase 'history repeats itself' came to his mind. It was immediately followed by an idea so startling that he found that he was holding his breath . . .

Some minutes later he got up and walked out of the room and down the corridor to Superintendent Crook-shank's office. He found him in conversation with his chief constable. There were empty coffee cups on the desk and both men were smoking. Pollard looked down at their enquiring faces through a thin blue haze.

'Come along in,' Henry Landfear invited. 'Is the Yard about to make an arrest or just continuing with its enquiries? Anything we can do?'

Pollard drew up a chair and sat down.

'Well, there's a bit of information you could give me off the cuff,' he said. 'Miss Grant's death last year was sudden, wasn't it?'

As he expected, astonishment was followed by a slight caginess.

'Yes,' Henry Landfear replied laconically. 'She fell off a ladder while she was tying up some climbing roses, and fractured her skull. The actual cause of death was intracranial haemorrhage.'

'Were you' – Pollard hesitated fractionally – 'absolutely satisfied with the verdict of accidental death?'

'What the hell—' Henry Landfear broke off and began again, speaking with deliberation. 'To answer your question. Yes, we were. Perfectly satisfied. She suffered from Ménière's disease, and her balance was liable to be disturbed. Of course she shouldn't have climbed ladders at all, but she was a strong-minded woman and didn't believe in wrapping herself up in cotton wool. From the position of the body on the ground it was clear that she had been reaching too far to one side, lost her balance, and fallen. Her watch was broken in the fall, and had stopped at five past two. There was no one else in the house. The nephew and niece who inherited the bulk of her estate were both out, and had witnesses to confirm their whereabouts. The daily woman had left before lunch as usual, and was at a Women's Fellowship meeting. Peter Grant found the body when he came home from the office at a quarter past five. In view of all this the verdict was a foregone conclusion.'

'Why I'm asking about it,' Pollard said, deciding to ignore the defensiveness that had built up, 'is that there's now no reasonable doubt that George Akerman was responsible for the death of the chap whose skeleton turned up in the kistvaen. Things have moved fast in the last twenty-four hours, and I was just waiting for official confirmation that he changed his car soon after Easter last year before putting you into the picture. The death probably took place at the Wanton Wenches stone circle at the Biddle end of Cattesmoor, and Akerman brought the body in his car to Starbarrow Farm and hid it in an old well-shaft. It was when the Lings were away. Incidentally, Ling has admitted finding the skeleton and parking it in the kistvaen. I don't believe that it was deliberate murder on Akerman's part, but I'm fairly sure that he had plans for his future which made it vital that he shouldn't be charged with manslaughter, for instance.'

Defensiveness on the part of the local men was replaced by stupefaction.

'*Akerman?*' Henry Landfear exclaimed. 'It's incredible! And anyway, how the devil does Heloise Grant's death come into it?'

'Suppose Davina Grant and Akerman were going to marry, and try to step into her local status while living at Upway Manor? If I'm right, her elimination was the first step.'

'*First* step?'

'Well, don't these anonymous letters and the phoney phone call look rather like an attempt to implicate Peter Grant in the skeleton affair, anyway to the extent of getting him talked about, so that he might decide to clear out of the area, and agree to sell his share of the house to Davina?'

A long uneasy silence developed.

'Remember that bastard Worth writing in the *Advertiser* when the Friends of Cattesmoor were electing a new president to follow Miss Grant?' Crookshank asked suddenly. 'Something about it being a surprise in certain quarters where it seemed to have been taken for granted that the job would be hereditary.'

Pollard suddenly realised that it was Crookshank's earlier remark about Worth's journalistic activities that he had subconsciously wanted to follow up.

'I remember your saying that he wrote malicious articles,' he said. 'Was he just enjoying having a dig at Davina Grant, do you think, or could he have suspected something offbeat about the aunt's death?'

'If Worth had any suspicions of Davina Grant or Akerman or anybody else he certainly wouldn't have left it at that,' Henry Landfear replied, looking worried. 'It's simply that he's a chap with an uncanny nose for people's weak spots, and enjoys drawing attention to them. I can't deny that he's sometimes been useful to us, without realising it, of course. No doubt the girl behaved tactlessly, and that gave him a handle ... Look here, Pollard, just what do you want done? I honestly can't see that you've unearthed anything at all that would justify reopening the enquiry into Heloise Grant's death.'

'Absolutely fair comment,' Pollard agreed. 'All I'm asking is to see the verbatim report of the inquest, and that if I stumble on anything that seems suggestive, you'll discuss it.'

They conceded that this was reasonable.

In the event all the relevant records were handed over, including the signed statements of everyone interviewed in connection with Heloise Grant's death, and a number of photographs of the south front of Upway Manor. With an unexpected flash of imagination Superintendent Crookshank provided an electric fan which made Pollard and Toye's small room more tolerable in the remorseless heat of midsummer, 1976. In spite of this amenity they found their long stint of concentrated mental effort taxing.

Gradually a picture of the events of 20 May 1975 emerged. For Pollard with his knowledge of their setting it was a vivid one. The morning had been perfectly normal and uneventful. Peter Grant had fetched Mrs Broom, the daily help, from Stoneham, before setting off again for his office. She had carried out her ordinary domestic work, with Heloise and Davina taking their usual share of the chores. Later in the morning Heloise had settled down to paperwork at her desk. At midday Davina had driven Mrs Broom back to Stoneham, and then returned to the snack lunch which she and her aunt always had, the household's main meal of the day being in the evening when Peter was home from the office. When questioned, Mrs Broom had said that Heloise Grant seemed just as usual; Davina, on the other hand, thought she looked tired, and said she had advised against the afternoon's gardening her aunt had planned to do.

'Naturally she'd tell the police that if she'd got a fake accident lined up,' Pollard observed, taking a gulp of a cold drink provided by the canteen. 'However, let's press on.'

After lunch, according to Davina, her aunt had gone to the drawing room with the day's *Times* for a rest. She herself had gone up to her bedsitter to get ready for her afternoon session at the Stoneham museum, where she did two stints of voluntary duty each week. A visit by a party of school-children had been booked for two o'clock, so she had left home in good time, coming downstairs just after half-past one. She found that her aunt had already gone into the garden, and brought an aluminium ladder from the gardener's shed and propped it against the front of the house, in order to tie up some sprays of the climbing roses loosened by a recent high wind. A further effort to get Heloise to take the afternoon quietly was laughed at, and she was told not to fuss. Davina drove to the museum where her presence from roughly 1.45 to 5.10 was vouched for by the caretaker and numerous other witnesses. On leaving she had gone to the Rectory with a message from her aunt. By chance she had mentioned to the caretaker that she had a call to make there before going

118

home, and so her brother had been able to ring her at about half-past five and tell her to go at once to the hospital where Heloise had been taken by ambulance.

'Foolproof, from the moment she left the Manor, wouldn't you say?' Toye asked.

Pollard agreed.

'Cast-iron, If there's a weak spot, it's not here.'

Peter Grant's alibi was equally unbreakable. He had lunched with a friend in a bar, and spent the entire afternoon working on plans in his office, seen at intervals by his secretary and other members of the staff. After knocking off at five o'clock he had driven straight home, and been appalled to discover his aunt lying on the gravel drive at the foot of the ladder. He had at once dialled 999 for an ambulance and managed to contact Davina at the Rectory by first ringing the museum.

'Equally cast-iron,' Pollard commented. 'He's obviously out of it. So is Mrs Broom. She turned up at the Parish Church Hall with a pal at about two-twenty, having had a bit of dinner with the said pal on coming back from her morning job.'

The investigations by the police had been thorough. An important clue to what had happened was a length of green garden string. One end was attached to a loose spray of a climbing rose well to the right of the ladder, while the other hung loose. The angle at which the body was lying was consistent with Heloise Grant's having leant well over to the right to tie the spray to a nail in the wall. The impact of her fall had slightly shifted the ladder, which was found to be a little crooked. It was in perfect condition and very steady, and carried numerous impressions of her fingerprints, and some less well-defined specimens of her gardener's, but no others. As she reached the ground, her left wrist and hand had struck the large stones bordering the flower bed along the front of the house, breaking the glass and mainspring of her watch which had stopped at five minutes past two. The watch was otherwise in perfect order, and had recently been cleaned and certified as keeping perfect time by Mr Robert Dell, horologist, of Stoneham. She was dead on arrival at the hospital. A postmortem examination had found the cause of death to be a severe intra-cranial haemorrhage resulting from a fractured skull, the time of death being estimated as between three and four hours previously. As she had been lying in the sun, it was difficult to be more exact, the pathologist had stated.

At the inquest Heloise Grant's doctor had stated that while in general her health was good, she suffered from Ménière's disease, and was liable to attacks in which her physical balance was affected. He had repeatedly advised her to avoid heights and all activities in which a loss of balance would be dangerous. She had not, however, paid much attention to these warnings, being a strong character and temperamentally averse to what she called 'giving in' to her disability. She certainly should not have climbed a ladder to any appreciable height.

The coroner had summed up at considerable length, giving due emphasis to all the main points which had emerged in evidence. He also gave due weight to the possibility of some unknown person having come into the garden of Upway Manor while Heloise Grant was on the ladder attending to the roses. She could have been startled by someone calling out, turned to see who it was, and in so doing lost her balance and fallen. If such a person had been an acquaintance, he or she had not come forward in spite of all the publicity. Moreover, it was impossible to believe that anyone in this category witnessing the fall would not have taken immediate steps to get medical aid. Mr Peter Grant had found the front door of the house standing open, and it would have been a matter of moments to reach a telephone. A more remote possibility was that someone with criminal intent had arrived on the scene with robbery in mind, and had threatened Heloise Grant by shaking or trying to move the ladder. Against this was the fact that the only fingerprints on the ladder were her own and her gardener's, and the absence of any signs of the ladder having been shifted, apart from the small dislodgement which could be attributed to the impact of her fall. After due consideration of all these matters, the coroner had concluded, the only reasonable verdict on Heloise Grant's fatal fall was one of Accidental Death . . .

Pollard pushed the papers aside.

'Some unknown person,' he quoted.

'Akerman?' Toye queried.

'On our theory it's possible. He was on visiting terms with Heloise Grant, so there'd have been nothing out of the ordinary in his turning up. But I'm sure he couldn't have come out by car or even on foot along Pilgrim Lane without somebody remembering afterwards. Her death must have been the Event of the Year in Stoneham. I suppose he might have approached the house from Cattesmoor, but how could Davina have contacted him and got everything fixed? Heloise Grant said she was going to garden in the course of the morning but no one could have known exactly when she'd have been tackling the roses ... No, on the whole I think the odds are that Davina did the job herself. It was probably all lined up, and she waited for a suitable opportunity.'

'Just exactly how was it done without leaving any dabs on the ladder, do you think?'

'Well, try to picture the scene. Heloise Grant's on the ladder, busy with tying up the roses. Davina comes out of the house and stands talking. Asking something about the message she's taking to the Rectory, perhaps. She points out a branch on her aunt's right which has come adrift. As Heloise leans over to cope with it, Davina slips a nylon cord around one of the rungs of the ladder, steps back and heaves with all she's got. A normal woman feeling a ladder coming adrift under her might be able to save herself if there was anything to grab, but not one liable to Ménière's disease. She loses her balance and crashes. Davina lets the ladder right itself. No need to touch it with her hands, and the nylon cord won't leave any recognisable mark on an aluminium rung. You can't see the front of the house from the lane, and she knows that the chance of anyone arriving at the critical moment is negligible. So she gets busy with changing the time of the watch on her aunt's wrist.'

Toye took off his horn rims, extracted a small piece of wash leather from their case, and polished them carefully. Pollard rubbed his eyes, tired from continuous reading, pushed back his chair and clasped his hands behind his head.

'Well, we've had it,' he said. 'There's not one bloody

thing we can put forward that would justify reopening the enquiry into Heloise Grant's death, is there? At least, not one that we've managed to spot ... All the same, I shall always feel certain that Davina managed to engineer the fall and get away with it ... Our deadline for meeting the C.C. and Crookshank's nine o'clock, so I suppose we'd better go and get something to eat first. It's about half-past six, isn't it? I thought I heard six strike just now.'

He stretched, flexed his left arm and looked at his watch.

'Half-past seven,' Toye said, consulting his own.

'It can't be!' Pollard put his watch to his ear, shook it and frowned. 'Hell! It's stopped. I dropped it on my bedroom floor this morning, but it seemed all right. I suppose I've bust the mainspring. I'll have to—'

He broke off, still staring at the watch, and sat completely immobile and oblivious of his surroundings for several seconds. As if unaware of what he was doing he took it off, and placed it carefully on the table. Suddenly he looked up at Toye, a grin dawning on his face.

'God!' he said. 'How exquisitely simple! How in the name of all that's holy has everyone missed it, ourselves included? There were *two* watches, of course. One was smashed by the fall, soon after one o'clock, I should think. The other had previously been deliberately dropped and smashed, and its hands put to five minutes past two. Change 'em over, get rid of the first one, and Bob's your Uncle ... But can it be proved?'

Chapter 10

It was at Superintendent Crookshank's suggestion that Mrs Broom was induced to come round to the police station when she returned from Upway Manor on the following morning. Reliable daily women, he maintained, and she must be one of those since she'd worked up there for years, often knew a damn sight more about what was in the house than their employers did.

She was understandably apprehensive, and sat bolt

upright in his office in her overall, clutching a shopping bag on her lap just as she had in Peter Grant's car when Pollard had first seen her. She was hatless, and had fuzzy mousy hair with some grey streaks and conspicuous dentures. He put her age at about fifty-five. She gave him the impression of having a mind of her own but of being chary of expressing it, as if you needed to be on your guard against life. As a working-class widow it probably hadn't been a bed of roses for her . . .

'Nice of you to come along to see us, love,' Crookshank was saying, jollying her along with an expertise which astonished Pollard. 'Of course you've been reading in the *Advertiser* about the rum things that've been going on in these parts, haven't you? Skeletons turning up in old monuments up on Cattesmoor and whatever?'

Mrs Broom looked baffled and nodded dumbly.

'And I expect you know that these two gentlemen from Scotland Yard have come down to help us sort it all out?'

She nodded again and murmured barely audible assent.

'Perhaps you remember me, Mrs Broom?' Henry Landfear came in. 'I used to visit Miss Grant at the Manor.'

At this she brightened up.

'Yes, sir, I remember you very well. Miss Grant had a lot of callers, what with all the committees she was on and the good she did. She's sorely missed, I'm told.'

'Quite true. And you must miss her yourself. She valued you, I know. Remembered you in her will, didn't she?'

'That's right, sir, and very grateful I was.'

'But you've stayed on to work for Miss Davina Grant?'

Mrs Broom hesitated briefly.

'I felt I owed it to Miss Grant, her being so good to me.'

'Now, love, there's something we want to ask you,' Crookshank told her. 'Anything you say here's one hundred per cent private, as if you were telling Father Mulley your sins in the confessional down at the Church, so you needn't be afraid to speak out. Tell us this. Were you quite easy in your mind about the verdict on Miss Grant's death in the coroner's court?'

Pollard watched her workworn hands tighten on the handles of the shopping bag until the knuckles showed white.

'That I wasn't,' she said at last, her voice unexpectedly shrill.

'Why not, Mrs Broom?' Henry Landfear asked quietly.

'Well, sir, for one thing Miss Grant wasn't looking poorly that morning, whatever Miss Davina said. She was joking and laughing while I was doing the drawing room, and talking about all the jobs she was going to do in the garden in the afternoon.'

'And for another thing?'

She hesitated once again, and then suddenly burst into rapid speech.

'She'd never have bin wearin' that watch. Not her best one for working in the garden, the one Miss Davina wears all the time now. Real valuable, she once told me it was. Solid gold, with her initials H.R.G. in tiny little pearls on the back. She'd always take it off for any messy work. Not that she did much o' that except for the garden, and that by her own choice, she bein' so wrapped up in it. But wear her best watch and risk gettin' the dirt in it, no never. She was a careful lady, Miss Grant was, and looked after her things proper for all she was so rich.'

'Do you mean, Mrs Broom, that she didn't wear a watch at all when she was gardening?' Pollard asked, breaking a tense silence.

'Oh, no, sir, I didn't mean that. She was a very punctual lady, and always had an eye to the time. She'd put on her silver watch for workin' in the garden. The one Miss Davina's given me. She had it put right first as it wasn't goin' well, she said. I won't say she hasn't bin generous in her way. I had a lovely coat of Miss Grant's too, and a big handbag – real leather.'

'You must value that watch a lot,' Henry Landfear remarked. 'Are you wearing it now, by any chance?'

Proudly she shot her left wrist clear of the sleeve of her overall, and showed him an old-fashioned silver watch on a grey leather strap.

'I always wears it except when I'm working, like Miss Grant did her gold one.'

'If you didn't believe that she was wearing the gold one for gardening the afternoon she was killed, why didn't you tell me when I came to see you?' Crookshank asked her.

'I didn't know nothing about what watch she was wearing, not till they said at the inquest. And seein' how the coroner put me down when I told 'im Miss Grant was well that mornin', sayin' Miss Davina was best placed to know, I thought I'd keep mum, and so I have, right up to this.'

'Caution to coroners,' Crookshank remarked to nobody in particular. 'Now then, ducks, here's the crunch. We want you to lend us your silver watch for a short time. Only till tonight, it could be. Take it from us, it'll be safe and sound. We'll give you a receipt for it. Don't look so worried. Our policemen are wonderful, you know. All the foreigners say so. We just want whoever cleaned it to take a look at it.'

At this Mrs Broom looked slightly less unhappy.

'That'll be Mr Dell down to Market Lane, for sure. He sees to the Manor clocks. Real valuable some of 'em, he told me once.'

She reluctantly unfastened the strap and handed over the watch.

'Here's your receipt,' Crookshank said. 'You'll get it back in a nice little box as soon as we've done with it.'

'You must have more to do up at the Manor these days,' Henry Landfear said casually. 'Miss Davina Grant's trying to carry on with all the things her aunt used to do, isn't she? The hospital Comforts Fund and the Friends of Cattesmoor and so on?'

'She'll never manage it,' Mrs Broom replied decisively. 'She isn't the woman her auntie was, not by a long chalk. Miss Grant had it all at her finger ends. Real businesslike she was, and that way she got it all done. Now Miss Davina's runnin' from pillar to post trying to catch up with herself. Up till two o'clock this morning writin' letters, she said she was, and then off to Wintlebury to some wholesale place for the Summer Fête stalls soon as I got to work this mornin'. That's three times she's trailed all the way up there these last few days, and all the stuff she's brought back locked up in one of the bedrooms, if you please. Why, in all the years I worked for Miss Grant never did she once turn a key on anythin', knowin' me like she did. And Miss Davina's off to a meetin' tonight, after she gets back. Real irritable she is, tryin' to fit it all in. I'll be properly thankful when the blessed Fête's over.'

Henry Landfear was suitably sympathetic.

'Well, we mustn't keep you from your dinner any longer, Mrs Broom,' he said. 'Thank you for coming along here and being so helpful.'

A constable was summoned and instructed to show her out.

'Surely she'll soon begin to wonder what all this has been in aid of?' Pollard asked, when the door had closed again.

'Her type and generation – down here, at least – is still inclined to write off the powers that be as incomprehensible,' Henry Landfear replied. 'But when she's had time to mull it over, she's sure to start talking to her cronies, so the sooner she gets her watch back, the better. What's your plan of action, Crookshank?'

'Start with Dell, sir, and hope to God that's where the watch was taken for repairs. If not, I suppose there'll have to be a circular to watch-repairers all over the country asking for details of what was wrong with it.'

'Shall we be any further on if somebody reports that it had a broken mainspring, though? It couldn't be proved that it was smashed deliberately,' Pollard said.

'You seem to have unearthed the perfect crime, don't you?' Henry replied gloomily. 'Unfortunately it's our case, not yours. What are you going to do about Akerman?'

'I know we've now got official confirmation that he had a new car in May '75, but I'd still like to wait for his back history before we move. I've been on to the Yard this morning, and we ought to hear something early this afternoon. The problem is what the charge against Akerman had better be.'

After a lengthy discussion over sandwiches and coffee it was agreed that Pollard and Toye should interview Robert Dell, and that a further conference should be held at half-past four. In the meantime enquiries would be made about the meeting Davina Grant and George Akerman were attending, and when they might reasonably be expected to return to Upway Manor.

After hearing that Robert Dell was a rum little guy but a marvel with clocks and watches, Pollard had unconsciously formed a mental picture of a Disney workshop, and was surprised to walk into a small up-to-date establishment in

126

Market Lane, presided over by a blonde with shoulder-length hair and violet eye shadow. The shelves were crowded with all types of modern clocks, from the severely functional to the grotesquely ornamental. Before he could speak, a deafening cacophony of whirring, wheezing, striking and explosive cuckooing announced three o'clock.

'You don't notice it once you're used to it,' the blonde reassured them. 'You gentlemen wanting a clock?'

'Not today, thank you,' Pollard replied. 'We'd like a word with Mr Dell, if he's here.'

'He's in the workshop,' she replied doubtfully, with a backward jerk of her head. 'What name shall I say?'

Pollard handed her his official card. Her mouth fell open, and with a strangled sound she vanished through a door behind her. They waited, contemplating the stock. Pollard pointed out a brick red plastic squirrel with protruding eyes which supported a clock face between its front paws.

'Like me to buy you that one?' he asked.

Before Toye could answer the blonde reappeared still open-mouthed.

'Will you step this way, please?'

The workshop at least was traditional in appearance. It had a bench with an apparent confusion of tools, and a number of disembowelled clocks in the process of being repaired. A large leather-bound ledger occupied a table in a corner. As well as taking all this in at first glance, Pollard spotted a superb grandfather clock.

'I keep him in here with me,' said a quiet voice from somewhere in the neighbourhood of his elbow. 'It's no place for him out in the shop with all the tinpot rubbish folks buy these days.'

Pollard looked down into a pair of bright brown eyes set in a wrinkled rosy face. Mr Dell was about four foot ten, with a perfectly bald cranium encircled by a ragged fringe of white hair.

'Mr Robert Dell?' he said. 'Good Lord, it's one of Thomas Tompion's?'

'It is, sir. And not for sale. Not for all the oil in the Middle East,' the little man added with startling modernity. 'You have come about stolen property, perhaps? Pray be seated, and the other gentleman, too.'

Pollard sat down on a battered upright chair. Mr Dell's face, he decided, was both childlike and extremely sagacious.

'No,' he replied. 'It's nothing to do with stolen property. I've come on a very confidential matter.'

Mr Dell bowed without speaking.

'I won't beat about the bush,' Pollard went on. 'I'm quite sure you know why I'm in Stoneham: to enquire into the finding of that skeleton on Cattesmoor. Police enquiries sometimes lead one in very unexpected directions ... I think you have done work for the late Miss Heloise Grant of Upway Manor for a good many years, haven't you?'

'And for her parents before her, sir.'

'I understand that the watch which she was wearing when she was killed was afterwards brought to you to be repaired?'

'That is correct,' Mr Dell replied. 'As it was broken by her fall and registered the time when this took place, I was closely questioned about its condition by the police. I was able to inform them that the damage done was consistent with the poor lady's fall, and that I had recently cleaned and regulated it for her. It was a beautiful piece of craftsmanship, and kept virtually perfect time. I may add that I was surprised that she was wearing it for gardening as she valued it so much. It is all too easy to knock a wristwatch when one is engaged in manual work. And there is the risk of it being damaged by water or some noxious substance.'

In the ensuing pause the grandfather clock chimed the first quarter. As the mellow notes died away Mr Dell smiled happily at Pollard.

Pollard smiled back, and took a small box from his briefcase.

'Do you recognise this?' he asked, holding out Mrs Broom's watch.

Mr Dell took it, scrutinised it, and opened the back for further inspection.

'This watch also belonged to the late Miss Grant,' he said. 'I have cleaned and regulated it for her from time to time. It is not in the same class as the other, of course, but very good of its kind and a reliable time-keeper.'

'When was it last brought in to you?'

Without answering Mr Dell got up and went over to the ledger. As he stood by the table turning over pages Pollard and Toye exchanged glances. In the enveloping silence the gentle remorseless ticking of a clock marked the passage of one second after another.

'This watch,' Mr Dell announced, 'was brought in to me by Miss Davina Grant in person on the afternoon of Monday, 4 August, last year. It was collected by her on Wednesday, 3 September, in response to a postcard informing her that it was ready. I dislike the telephone intensely,' he added, returning to his chair.

'What repairs had you done to it?'

'Miss Davina Grant informed me that shortly before she died her aunt had dropped it on the stone floor of the scullery while washing her hands after gardening. The glass and the mainspring were both broken and the winder was missing. The poor lady was a great gardener. I understood that this watch was to be given to the daily woman as a memento of her late mistress.'

'What a wonderful memory you have,' Pollard told him. 'It's astonishing that you can remember all this detail when so many watches must pass through your hands. Why, it's almost a year ago.'

Mr Dell gave the slow secretive smile of a child hugging a delectable memory.

'I'll always remember Monday, 4 August 1975,' he said. 'My grandson was born that day. Five little girls my daughter'd had, and we were on tenter-hooks, my wife and I. My son-in-law had only telephoned an hour before Miss Davina came in with that watch. And talk about coincidence: the watch had stopped at twenty minutes past one, the very moment the little lad came into this world.'

As Pollard and Toye commented a little incoherently, Mr Dell's expression slowly became less childlike and more sagacious.

'Gentlemen of your standing, sir, don't come around asking questions about watch repairs unless it's an important matter. I can't see what the ones you've been asking

129

me are leading to, but it's the sort of thing makes a man uneasy.'

'Unfortunately, Mr Dell,' Pollard replied, 'in our job we can't avoid making a lot of people uneasy. Not that you personally have anything to worry about, I need hardly say. It's possible you may be asked to make a formal statement about this watch. If it is, you'll hear from Superintendent Crookshank. Thank you for the information you've given us, and now we won't take up any more of your time.'

A couple of minutes later they were walking back to the police station along Market Lane.

'Why didn't she shift the hands?' Toye asked. 'If the winder had come adrift and disappeared in a flower bed when Miss Grant fell, surely she could have got hold of another?'

'Not as easy as it sounds without making yourself conspicuous. It's an old watch, remember, and winders aren't standardised. And obviously by August she was over-confident. The inquest was over, and everything nicely rounded off. No questions asked about the gold watch, except whether it was reliable, and Dell had testified to that. So 1.20 was no more significant than any other time. The yarn about Miss Grant having a wash in the scullery as she came into the house is the commonplace sort of thing that's so convincing. But I think she tripped up over the time. Their normal lunch hour was one o'clock, and according to Mrs Broom Miss Grant was a very punctual lady. Would she have come in unwashed twenty minutes late?'

Toye considered.

'You've got some points, there. But what Dell's given us isn't what you'd call conclusive, is it? Do you think they'll charge her, all the same?'

'I don't know. They're rattled, and I don't wonder, poor chaps. Anyway, it's their business, not ours, thank the Lord.'

Pollard spoke with enough vehemence to get a quick glance from Toye. As they walked in silence he faced the fact that he was feeling rattled himself, and wondered why. Whatever the Yard had managed to unearth about George

Akerman could hardly affect the case against him. The identity of the skeleton had not been discovered and probably never would be, but surely Akerman's involvement in the chap's death and the concealment of the body was beyond doubt? And Geoffrey Ling had admitted to the fool's trick of moving the skeleton to the kistvaen ... After all, Pollard told himself, that was the job I was sent down here to do, and I've done it.

It was not until they were going up the steps of the police station that he realised that his uneasiness was in connection with Davina Grant.

He was temporarily distracted by the report on George Akerman which had come through. He was of working-class origin, won a free place at a grammar school and had been apprenticed to a printer. His war record had been satisfactory, if undistinguished, and he had subsequently had a job with a printing firm in South London. At the age of thirty he had married a girl ten years younger than himself, who had left him for another man a year later. He had divorced her, sold the house which he had been buying through a building society, and disappeared from London with a few thousand pounds left him by an uncle.

'Well, we can fill in the rest,' Pollard said. 'An entirely new pattern of life emerges. He turns up in Stoneham, buys a moribund printing works, and settles down to make a success of it and play a part in local affairs, especially on the conservation side. He develops archaeological interests, and starts moving in quite a different social circle. At the same time he lives an oddly solitary sort of life.'

'On the up and up, that's plain enough,' Toye commented.

'Heading for what? Our theory is marriage with Davina Grant and living at Upway Manor. But you know, the more I think of it, the more unbelievable it seems that a chap like Akerman could think the game worth the candle ... that hopelessly immature stupid girl would drive him round the bend, surely . . .'

Pollard's voice trailed off.

Toye looked at him enquiringly.

'There's something pretty chilling about the way Akerman dealt with that body, isn't there? I'm beginning

131

to wonder if his long-term plan included a fatal accident for Davina? However, I suppose all this is beside the point, as we're bringing his little game to a full stop . . . Come on, we're due with the C.C. and Crookshank.'

Of all the frustrating cases I've ever had, Pollard thought, as they walked along an echoing corridor smelling of disinfectant. Hopelessly tangled up with what looks like a perfect murder . . .

It was as he arrived at Superintendent Crookshank's door that a possible joint course of action sprang into his mind.

Chapter 11

At the end of Pollard's account of his visit to Robert Dell, Henry Landfear and Superintendent Crookshank exchanged expressive looks.

'Yes,' Crookshank said gloomily. 'That's how it was done, all right. No doubt at all.'

Henry Landfear agreed, stubbing out a cigarette end in an already over-full ashtray.

'No doubt and no proof,' he said with finality. 'Can't you hear the whole business about the watches being torn to shreds in court, always supposing the D.P.P. would let the case go forward?'

As Pollard remained silent, he looked at him challengingly.

'Hell! Would you charge Davina Grant with her aunt's murder on the evidence we've got?'

'Not on the evidence we've got at the moment.'

'I'm not with you.'

'I'd try shock tactics to get some more. All according to the book, of course.'

'Well, if you've got any practicable suggestions, let's have 'em, by all means.'

'O.K.,' Pollard replied, astonished by the speed at which his mind had been working, even while he was recounting the interview with Robert Dell. 'Quite a simple plan has occurred to me. We know that Davina Grant and Akerman are going back to Upway Manor for supper after their meeting this evening, and that Peter Grant's going out with Kate Ling. We've got a warrant for Akerman's arrest on a charge of murdering the hippy. You get one for Davina's arrest. Both of them are overconfident. It's a year and over since the two deaths, and no questions asked, and they're in a state of mind which makes people highly vulnerable to unexpected accusations. We arrive at the Manor, take them by surprise, and I charge Akerman. If he keeps his head and neither of them will talk, you – the Stoneham team – are as you were. You don't execute your warrant, that's all. But from the impression I've formed of Davina Grant I think she'll go to pieces. She's crazy about Akerman, and she's 'a very stupid, if cunning, young woman. The whole thing may end in their going for each other: it wouldn't surprise me if Akerman's real feelings about her burst out. If this sort of fracas develops I think it's highly probable that they'll give themselves away, and it'll be up to us to freeze on to anything relevant that's said.'

During the silence that followed he watched Henry Landfear and Crookshank stare at him, digest his proposal, and then, to their own surprise, recognise that there could be something to it. Crookshank, weighed down with the sense of having failed in the original enquiry into Heloise Grant's death, was the first to speak.

'I take your point,' he said. 'All of 'em, come to that. As you say, we don't stand to lose if it doesn't come off.'

'What I'm thinking about is what we're going to look like if it does come off,' Henry Landfear said heavily, 'seeing that we seem to have missed out completely over Heloise Grant.'

'Surely,' Pollard replied, 'it won't be the first time that fresh evidence turns up about a murder in the course of an investigation into something else?'

Henry Landfear suddenly grinned, relieving the tense atmosphere.

'You're a good sort, Pollard. Well, what about it, Crookshank, if you're game? It's O.K. by me. Where do we go from here? Time's short.'

'Better find out what time the meeting they're going to starts, hadn't we?'

'That's easy. My wife's on the Friends of Cattesmoor committee. I'll ring her right away...'

The meeting, they learnt, was to begin at half-past five. After some discussion it was settled that Pollard, Toye, Crookshank and support should go up in two cars at half-past six, and park farther up the hill, just out of sight of the entrance to Upway Manor, in the lane leading to Cattesmoor.

'After that,' Pollard said, 'it'll be a case of playing it by ear. Waiting on events and whatever.'

Shortly afterwards they dispersed to get a hasty meal before going into action. Back at their hotel Pollard and Toye collected sandwiches and beer and made for a table in a corner of the bar. As they ate they talked intermittently.

'I'd have wanted a month of Sundays to get this scheme worked out,' Toye said.

'The idea hit me just as we got to the Super's door. Now, of course, I'm getting cold feet.'

'You mean you're afraid they won't talk, and it'll be a washout as far as the girl goes?'

'Not quite. It's the feeling I've had all along that we haven't got to the bottom of things. What really sparked off that skeleton business. As if even now something could pop out and hit me... Anyway, we're committed to going ahead over Akerman. Have another pie – I've tasted worse. It may be some time before we get a chance of any more grub.'

As they ate they intermittently followed a TV news programme. Local items considered newsworthy by the producer flicked on and off the screen. A fat woman was interviewed about an alleged poltergeist in her cottage. The public were warned about faulty electric light bulbs included in a consignment of Suntraps delivered to local shops. A group of villages were lobbying County Hall about the inadequacy of their refuse collections...

'Finished?' Pollard asked. 'Let's push off, then.'

Punctually at half-past six Crookshank, a sergeant, and a constable drove off from the carpark at the police station. Pollard, Toye and a second constable followed at an interval of ten minutes, it having been agreed that to go in convoy was unnecessarily conspicuous. At Upway Manor Toye turned the Rover in the drive entrance, and backed gingerly up the unsurfaced lane beyond.

'Cheer up,' Pollard encouraged him. 'It's only round the first bend.'

A wait of unknown duration now lay ahead. The sergeant and the constables had brought evening papers, and sat on the bank reading them. Crookshank moved to the back seat of the Stoneham car and became engrossed in official documents. Toye produced maps and studied the landscape over the gate. Pollard strolled on up the hill towards the moor, trying to recapture the atmosphere of his setting out on the Possel Way less than a fortnight earlier. He saw that even the countryside had perceptibly changed. The hedgerows had wilted under the blazing sun and were scattered with the petals of the wild roses, while the grasses were filmed with fine dust. The moor when he reached it now had a tawny scorched look, accentuated by the yellowing light of the evening sun. He stood for a few moments gazing westward along the route of the Possel Way. The track was inviting, compelling even, he thought, and wondered if something of the feelings of the pilgrims who had used it could possibly still hang about it. Reluctantly returning to the present he retraced his steps and joined the rest of the party. Crookshank looked up and gave him a brief nod as he passed.

Time dragged on interminably and a degree of tension began to make itself felt. Several people made an involuntary movement as a bird suddenly scuttered in the hedge. Shadows lengthened imperceptibly, and bright points of light began to stab the blue haze over Stoneham on the far side of the valley. Then, at long last, heads went up sharply. There was a moment of indecision followed by a slight stiffening as the sound of an approaching car became unmistakable. It increased to a level at which it was possible to distinguish two cars, and reached a climax as they slowed to turn into the drive. It died away rapidly and ceased. Two car doors slammed. There was an outburst of barking.

'Right,' Pollard said.

He led the way to the gates. The supporting Stoneham men faded into the shrubs bordering the short drive to the garage, while Toye and Crookshank followed him across the lawn in the direction of the house. As before there were lights in the drawing-room windows.

Suddenly Toye stopped dead.

'That's not Akerman's car outside the house. It's the B.M.W.,' he said.

Pollard had the feeling of the ground giving way under his feet, the sense of a premonition fulfilled increasing his dismay. He took a grip on himself as Crookshank swore under his breath, but before he could speak a male figure appeared at one of the windows and flung it up at the bottom.

'Hullo?' Peter Grant called enquiringly. 'Why, it's Superintendent Pollard! And Superintendent Crookshank . . . Nothing wrong, is there?'

'Good evening,' Pollard said, walking on ahead. 'We wanted a word with Mr Akerman, and we've been told that he's coming here to supper with your sister after a meeting in the town. I take it they haven't got back yet?'

'No, they haven't. I shouldn't think they'll be long. But do come in, won't you? I'll shut the dog in the kitchen.'

'Car,' mouthed Crookshank as they walked to the front door. Pollard nodded, as Peter Grant appeared on the step.

'Come in,' he said, looking put out. 'I'd no idea George Akerman was coming to supper. Rather tiresome. My fiancée and I wanted to discuss something with my sister, and had our own supper early. Kate's just making some coffee. You'll join us, won't you?'

He ushered them into the drawing room and vanished, saying something about extra cups. Crookshank was at the open window in a flash, giving a low whistle. His sergeant appeared.

'Move the small car out of sight round the back of the house. Not the B.M.W., the other. Sharp!'

He drew his head and shoulders in again abruptly, knocking over a small table sending unopened letters and a reading lamp flying, and swore once again as Toye hurried to pick them up.

136

'Put paid to the bulb, I suppose. Try it, will you?'

Toye pressed the switch without result, and began to examine the lamp to see if the bulb had worked loose in its socket. The next moment he put it down quickly and stooped to pull out the wall plug. Pollard and Crookshank stared at him in surprise.

'The bulb's a Suntrap,' he said half-apologetically. 'Best to be on the safe side after what we heard about 'em on the box just now.'

'Suntrap? Not the sort of cut-price job you'd expect to find in a house like this,' Crookshank commented.

'How long has the scare about faulty specimens been going on round here?' Pollard asked, conscious of a constriction in the region of his spine.

'Since the end of last week. Some turned up in shops in Wintlebury. We've put out warnings.'

The crunch of tyres on gravel came from outside. A quick glance from the window showed Kate Ling's Mini Clubman being competently manhandled. Voices and the clink of crockery sounded in the hall, and Kate Ling walked into the room carrying a cake on a plate, followed by Peter Grant with the coffee tray. She wore a long flowered skirt and a silk top of a blue that matched her eyes; she gave Pollard a radiant smile. It faded as she sensed the tension in the group by the window. Crookshank took a step forward.

'Sorry to sound abrupt, Mr Grant, but I want to know what make of electric bulb you normally use in this house.'

Peter Grant put down the tray and faced him incredulously.

'Vestas. I get them wholesale.' There was more than a trace of annoyance in his expression and voice. 'Just what is all this in aid of?'

'Do you ever use a brand called Suntrap?' Crookshank rapped out, disregarding the question.

'N-never heard of it,' Peter Grant retorted, stuttering slightly in rising indignation tinged with uneasiness.

Kate put her hand on his arm.

'I have,' she said. 'This evening, for the first time as it happens. There've been dangerous faulty ones, and there was a news flash on TV warning people.'

'We'll take a look at this particular specimen,' Crookshank announced.

Toye, already prepared for action with a handkerchief wrapped round his hand, removed the bulb from the reading lamp with extreme care and held it out for inspection.

'Is this the chair where you sit when you come in of an evening to open your mail and take a look at the paper, Mr Grant?' Crookshank asked.

'At this time of year, yes.'

'Then you and Inspector Toye here are a couple of bloody lucky chaps. See this bit of wire coming through the base of the bulb? Switch on the lamp and it becomes lethal. Fortunately I banged into the table and knocked everything over, smashing the bulb, and it led to our noticing the brand.'

Kate Ling's hold on Peter Grant's arm tightened. He suddenly burst into speech.

'Look here, I've had about enough of this. What the hell are you getting at? Nobody could put in that bulb without spotting the end of wire.'

'My point exactly, Mr Grant.'

In the pause which followed, the distant sound of an approaching car was heard. There was a sudden change of atmosphere as Pollard took over.

'Take Miss Ling into another room and stay with her there,' he ordered peremptorily. 'It's a police order,' he barked out as neither of them moved. 'Get cracking, do you hear?'

As if returning to life they turned and went, Peter's arm round Kate's shoulders as he steered her out of the room. Crookshank flung himself into the chair by the reading lamp and looked enquiringly at Pollard, who nodded approval and signed to Toye to come to the other end of the room. As two cars came down the drive and drew up outside the house, he looked down at Toye with a sense of inexpressible relief.

Car doors slammed successively. Davina Grant's girlish enthusiasm came through the open window.

'Oh, George, isn't it a *welcoming* old house after a long hard day? What's dear Mrs Broom got in the fridge for supper, I wonder? Peter!' she trilled. 'Here we are!'

A moment later she walked into the drawing room. Pollard saw her eyes fly to the chair. At the sight of Crookshank reclining in it she froze in her tracks. Her hand flew to her mouth in a clumsy involuntary gesture. George Akerman, immediately behind, almost collided with her.

'Not where you expected to find him, I take it?' Crookshank enquired coolly.

Her face darkened and became ugly with fury. Pollard came forward, pointedly ignoring her.

'George Akerman,' he heard himself saying. 'I hold a warrant for your arrest on a charge of murdering a man, whose identity is at present unknown, on 1 April last year. I warn you that anything you say will be taken down and may be used in evidence.'

For a moment no one spoke or moved. He identified a curious sound as Davina Grant breathing heavily. George Akerman's expression was impassive.

'I deny the charge,' he said mechanically. A slight movement behind him indicated that the three Stoneham men had moved in.

Davina Grant took a lunging step towards Pollard.

'You're mad! It's monstrous!' she spat at him. 'How *dare* you? I'm going to ring the Chief Constable.'

Turning to go out into the hall she found the way barred by uniformed men. Her name rang out from behind her. She swung round to find herself facing Crookshank.

'Davina Grant,' he repeated. 'I hold a warrant for your arrest on a charge of murdering Heloise Grant on 20 May 1975. I—'

The caution was lost in a peal of triumphant laughter.

'You can't prove it,' she mocked him.

The stunned silence which followed was broken at last by George Akerman.

'*You* killed *her?*'

The words dropped into the stillness like heavy stones into deep water.

Davina Grant gave a secretive complacent smile as she turned to him.

'You'd planned to marry her, hadn't you? I was watching ... I was afraid she might be hotting up a bit when you were seeing so much of each other over that stupid Possel Way ... What a silly man you are. Don't you see that I can give you everything she could have given, and a lot more?'

She leered at him.

With a swiftness of movement that took the encircling police off guard, George Akerman had her by the throat. Illumination flooded into Pollard's mind as he helped to drag him away.

The room was suddenly full of people, noise and shouted orders from Crookshank. George Akerman, limp and unresisting, offered no opposition to being handcuffed and led to a chair.

'Let me sit on the other side of the room,' he said unexpectedly.

'Why?' Pollard asked.

In reply he got a jerk of the head towards Heloise Grant's portrait.

'I'd like to look at that ... I shan't see it again.'

'Move him across,' Pollard said. 'And get the car, Toye, will you? We'll take him down to the station.'

Crookshank, looking preoccupied, came up.

'She's not badly hurt,' he said. 'The ambulance is on its way. Let it get through first, will you, as the lane's narrow. The young couple are following on to the hospital in their own car. I'm leaving a chap in charge up here for the moment ... Be seeing you later.'

George Akerman was informed of his legal rights but decided to send for a solicitor.

'I'll make a statement, if that's what you want,' he said dully. 'I'm not a murderer. I never touched him. I found him with a dirty great fire blazing up against one of the Wanton Wenches. I yelled at him and started to run, meaning to give the blighter a bashing. He took to his heels, suddenly crumpled up and crashed into one of the stones ... His face was just a bloody mess ...'

'You should have got him to the Biddle hospital at once.'

'No point. He'd had it. Heart, I suppose. I was an R.A.M.C. orderly in the war.'

'And this was on Tuesday, 1 April, last year, the day you said you spent at home?'

'Yes. When you started nosing into things the best thing seemed to be to switch the Monday and the Tuesday round, and hope that if anybody'd spotted me they wouldn't remember which day it was.'

'So you decided the chap was dead, and then lost your head completely, didn't you?' Pollard asked.

George Akerman continued to stare at the table.

'I was in love with Heloise Grant,' he said at last. 'What price my chances with a charge of culpable homicide or whatever you like to call it hanging over my head?'

Eventually a statement was put together and submitted to him. He made a show of reading it through, scrawled his name at the bottom, and listened to Pollard's information about the immediate future with a complete lack of interest.

'All the same to me,' he muttered. 'This time I've had it for good. Life packed up on me once before, and I decided to have another go. Not this time. And that's bloody well all I'm saying.'

He relapsed into obstinate silence. When he was escorted out of the room Pollard followed, returning after a few minutes.

'I've warned them to watch out,' he said, slumping down wearily. 'A suicide would just about round things off, wouldn't it? I suppose our job's worth it. Saving half the human race from the other half. They're either stupid or plain wicked. That woman Heloise Grant giving her life to local good works and never noticing what was festering in the girl's mind . . . I expect she'll get off. Unfit to plead, or something.'

Toye glanced at him and made a characteristically practical suggestion of getting a bit of sleep in what was left of the night.

They were stuffing papers into their briefcases when a constable arrived.

'Miss Ling would be glad of a word, sir,' he told Pollard. 'She's in Waiting Room C.'

'Miss Ling?' Pollard exclaimed. 'Still here? Good Lord, it's half-past two. We'll go along at once.'

Kate was alone, sitting at a table in the harsh glare of an unshaded electric light. She had thrown an old coat round her shoulders for warmth and there were dark shadows under her eyes, but she smiled as they came in, composed and even relaxed.

'Peter's on the line,' she said. 'The family solicitor's just rung him again. We felt we had to see you, Mr Pollard. I – I owe you Peter's life, don't I? And we want to say how immensely thankful we are that Inspector Toye's all right. That bit just doesn't bear thinking about.'

As Toye mumbled something about it being all in the day's work Peter Grant came in looking white and exhausted, but rather touchingly dignified, Pollard thought.

'. . . utterly shattering that I don't feel I've really taken it in properly,' he was saying. 'But do believe I'm grateful to you for bringing the whole ghastly business into the open. Suppose anything – anything else . . .'

'We're being married as soon as we can get a special licence,' Kate said firmly as she got up. 'I've told Peter that otherwise I'll break off our engagement,' she added, slipping her arm in his.

'Upway's the snag,' he said, drawing her close to him. 'Grants have lived there for the last couple of centuries, but I couldn't face it now.'

'I'm marrying you, not an eighteenth-century manor listed Grade B,' Kate remarked. 'Besides, you're an architect. We can start from scratch. Have a house we've thought up ourselves, and begin its history.'

'Ride out the storm here in Stoneham?'

'Here or anywhere. It's a wide, wide world. We'd better be going, don't you think? . . . Mr Pollard?'

'Yes, Miss Ling?' he said, wondering what was coming.

'Don't have too hard thoughts of Father. After all, if he hadn't done that crazy thing with the skeleton?' . . .

'Perfectly true,' Pollard told her. 'As a matter of fact it struck me while we've been talking.'

'Dare I tell you' – she gave him a sidelong glance – 'that he's already got there himself? I'm afraid he's quite irrepressible.'

On this more relaxed note they all went out to the car-park. It was still dark, but Pollard sensed a touch of dawn freshness in the air as he stood watching the B.M.W. drive off.

'Something salvaged,' Toye commented as its tail light vanished.

'All right, all right,' Pollard retorted. 'I'll admit to feeling a bit less jaundiced. Let's go.'

He smote Toye powerfully between the shoulder blades and they walked across to the Rover.